TREE OF LIFE

AN ARKANE THRILLER
J.F. PENN

Tree of Life. An ARKANE Thriller Book 11
Copyright © J.F.Penn (2020). All rights reserved.

www.JFPenn.com

ISBN: 978-1-913321-36-9

Requests to publish work from this book should be sent to:
joanna@CurlUpPress.com

Cover and Interior Design: JD Smith Design

Printed by Amazon KDP Print

www.CurlUpPress.com

"Now the Lord God had planted a garden in the east, in Eden; and there he put the man he had formed. The Lord God made all kinds of trees grow out of the ground — trees that were pleasing to the eye and good for food. In the middle of the garden were the tree of life and the tree of the knowledge of good and evil."

Genesis 2: 8-9

"Nature, red in tooth and claw."

Alfred, Lord Tennyson

"No tree, it is said, can grow to heaven unless its roots reach down to hell."

Carl Jung

PROLOGUE

A THOUSAND CANDLES LIT the synagogue of Ets Haim in Amsterdam, the light flickering in a warm glow from the copper chandeliers that hung over the bowed heads of the faithful. Some held candles in their hands, upturned faces full of hope and sorrow, and their prayers spiraled heavenward with the sweet smell of smoke.

The fine acoustics of the synagogue resounded with the songs of the choir, unique to this community, sung in Hebrew with Portuguese inflection. The lack of electric light made the place seem timeless, the faithful engaged in a tradition stretching back across the ages. Words spoken by generations long dead, whispered behind closed doors during times of persecution, and spoken aloud with pride during times of freedom.

Aaron Heertje usually loved Yom Kippur, the holiest day of the Jewish year, when the community came together to repent and atone for their sins. But this year, it was a time of dread — he was about to have far more to atone for.

Sweat dripped down Aaron's spine as he stood at the end of the wooden bench, his suit tight against his chest as he fought for each breath. His black top hat, worn by all men in the Portuguese Jewish community, sat like a heavy weight upon his head. He longed to pull it off, but he couldn't draw attention to himself. He wiped his brow and tried to calm his pounding pulse as the seconds ticked away.

The cantor came to the end of his song, the final note lingering before fading into silence. Men from the community carried the Torah scroll from the ark of Brazilian jacaranda wood, brought from Recife by Portuguese Jews returning to the safety of Amsterdam. The Rabbi stepped forward to read. He used a *yad*, a ritual pointer with a tiny hand on the end, to move across the scroll as he recited the ancient words that Jews had spoken for thousands of years.

As others around him listened intently, some with lips moving to the familiar sacred text, Aaron looked at his watch. He was out of time.

The gaze of the community remained fixed on the Rabbi as Aaron stepped out of his row and hurried to the back of the synagogue. The fine sand strewn across the floor softened the sound of his footsteps, a reference to the desert crossed by the Israelites as they fled from Egypt so long ago.

Aaron slipped quietly out the door and rushed past the workshop where the candles were made for holy days. As the chanting rose once more, it stifled the sound of his retreat. But there was no one out here to witness, anyway. All the faithful were inside, taking their place as members of the community. A community he was about to betray.

As he reached the door of the library, he looked at his watch again. Just ten more minutes and Rachel would be safe in his arms once more. Aaron could only hope that he would have a chance to atone for the sin he was about to commit, but surely, it was a greater sin to let a loved one die when there was a way to save that life.

He pulled a key from his pocket with a trembling hand, his fingers lingering on the rough texture of its handle. The Rabbi had given it to him two years ago in exchange for a solemn promise that he would keep these manuscripts as safe as he would the souls of his loved ones. But as much as

Aaron loved the word of God, he loved his wife more. All he had to do was give up one obscure fragment of a manuscript and she would be returned to him.

Perhaps no one would ever even know about it. After all, the Ets Haim Library held many thousands of books and hundreds of manuscripts, as well as countless fragments of ancient texts. Who would miss one tiny little piece?

Aaron pushed open the door and entered the library. The faint smell of cedar wood hung in the still air, a scent he always associated with this haven of learning. This place was akin to the Holy of Holies for those who loved words and who scoured the texts for ancient wisdom.

He held the candle high and his shadow cast a dark path ahead through the beam of light. In normal times, he would never bring an open flame in here, but the candle was safe in its holder and he dared not switch the lights on for fear of being seen.

The beam glanced over his allotted seat, the leather cushion worn and dented into the shape of his bony frame. It was not quite comfy enough to make study pleasant, but still, it had been his place in a sanctuary of learning reserved for true students. Scholars from all over the world tried hard to get a spot to study here, but it was almost impossible unless their credentials were well verified. Aaron had worked hard for that seat. Now it would be forever tainted by what he was about to do.

He pulled his phone from his pocket and opened the photo that had been texted to him last night. Rachel bound and gagged, her precious face bloody, her hazel eyes terrified — and a demand for a manuscript fragment with a specific library reference. Aaron had not recognized it, but then the library held so much and it would take many lifetimes to read every word it contained.

"Soon, my love," he whispered, the surrounding books the only witnesses to his pain.

Aaron put away his phone and walked over to the index, a huge leather-bound tome with handwritten entries, added to over the years as ancient manuscripts were retrieved from communities around the world. He placed the candle-holder down and pulled out the pair of white gloves he always wore to touch the texts before leafing through the pages.

The entry he needed lay within an area of the library infrequently visited. It held not holy books, but fragments of texts that resisted scholarship because they were incomplete. This one was unusual as it was marked with only one word, *Tuin*. Aaron frowned. It was the Dutch word for garden and yet everything else was catalogued with Hebrew or at least a mixture of Hebrew and Dutch.

The sound of the cantor drifted across the courtyard and his prayers gave Aaron pause. What was he really giving away this night?

The seconds ticked away.

He shook his head. Rachel was everything and even the Rabbi must agree that her life was worth much more than this fragment, whatever it might be.

Aaron turned to a different part of the index, leaving it open at a new page to hide his search. He picked up the candleholder once more and hurried to the back section of the library beyond the furthest shelves he had been allowed to study. This area was not exactly forbidden, but the junior members of the library rarely accessed it. If he remained at Ets Haim, Aaron could climb the ranks of scholars over the years and as he progressed, he would be allowed to read more. Such manuscripts were a worthy goal for study — and right now, he trespassed too soon. It was necessary, but his heart hammered as he took each step toward his goal.

A huge rack of drawers stood against the back wall, etched with Hebrew letters and numbers, and some with strange symbols carved upon them. Aaron ran his fingers lightly over the wood, his lips moving in a prayer. The drawer he sought was near the bottom of the case, its number matching the ransom text. But there was something else next to the reference code.

An ancient Jewish warning, a curse of some kind.

Aaron frowned. It was highly unusual. These words were infrequently used, and he had never seen them in the library, only in ancient texts from pagan, superstitious places. Never here in modern Amsterdam. Perhaps it remained from some historical use of the wood, or… Aaron shook his head and pushed the doubts aside.

He tugged at the drawer, but it didn't move. It was locked shut with no obvious place for a key. Panic rose inside as Aaron tried desperately to think where it might be and a hot flush washed over him as he thought of the ring of keys that the Rabbi carried at all times. Perhaps it was on his belt even now as he stood surrounded by the faithful in the hall… No, there had to be a way inside.

Aaron raised the candle higher and examined the drawers more carefully. There was no obvious keyhole, and sometimes the cabinetmakers created opening mechanisms in different places. He ran his fingers around the edge of the cabinet, feeling for any variation in the wood.

There, at the back of the base, a tiny catch.

He lifted it and heard a clunk from inside the drawers. Aaron knelt once more and pulled at the handles.

This time the drawer slid free, and he sighed with relief as he carefully eased it open. Some part of him expected to find something shocking or terrifying, something worthy of the curse protecting it. But inside, there were only three manuscript fragments encased in glass fitting snugly into the wooden drawer.

At first glance in the semi-darkness, they were nothing special, just more fragments in a library full of them. But as Aaron held the candle higher, he noticed that one of them looked unusual.

It was a fragment of a map rather than a manuscript, illustrated with tiny vines. He bent closer. No, they weren't vines; they were something else. There were hooks and razor-sharp barbs on the faded green swirls, and the crimson flowers that sprouted from them resembled open mouths dripping with poison. A tree stood behind the malevolent vines, part of its trunk visible on the fragment and intricately painted with strange symbols. Its leaves spread out across the page toward a deep river teeming with life. There were other markings on the edge of the map, but it was torn and ragged. This piece was perhaps one quarter of the original.

The tree gave Aaron pause. He stood within the Ets Haim Synagogue, named for the Tree of Life in the book of Genesis. Perhaps this image was the tree of which the scriptures spoke? But surely that was just a metaphor, and God did not cast mankind out of some physical Garden of Eden.

The fragment was beautiful and mysterious, precious for sure, but it was the price of Rachel's life and Aaron was more than willing to pay it.

A sound came from outside the library, a scuff of boots on stone.

It was time.

Aaron lifted out the glass case with the Eden fragment and moved the others over to cover the space. He closed the drawer and stood up, spinning around and holding the candle high.

Footsteps came from the outer library.

A tall figure moved into the doorway just out of the candle beam, his features obscured by the semi-darkness. Aaron could see the immense size of the man. He filled the low wooden doorway, a looming physicality in a library built for men of a more studious stature.

"Where is she?" Aaron stammered.

"The manuscript first," the man replied, his voice low and hoarse as if he had sustained some kind of throat injury and had to force his words out.

Aaron held up the glass case, his hand shaking a little. "It's only a fragment. This is all there is, I promise you."

The man took a step forward, and his presence seemed to fill the room.

Aaron shuffled away until his back rested against the shelves. They were in the furthest reaches of the library now. There was nowhere to run.

The candle shook in his hand as the man reached for the glass case.

"Tell me where she is. Please."

As the man stepped forward, the light of the candle revealed his face. The smoke turned his visage into something demonic with the hard planes of a fighter's chin and underneath, a ravaged neck with the scars of one who had faced battle and emerged with no pity.

Sometimes God sent an avenging angel, sometimes His plan unfolded through the hands of violent men and Aaron had a sudden sense that his own tree of life was ending. In Kabbalah, there was a moment when each spark of light was released back into the world as its physical container perished. As he looked into the man's eyes, Aaron understood that Rachel's spark was already free. Perhaps it was not the worst thing that he would soon join her.

The man snatched the Eden fragment away with one hand and with the other, he raised a heavy golden candlestick high in his meaty fist. The sound of voices chanting prayers of atonement came from the synagogue beyond, and in that last moment, Aaron joined in, the sacred words smashed from his lips as the weapon came down.

Pain exploded as he fell to the ground, palms raised in supplication. The candle in his hand rolled away, its light flickering as the man loomed over him. As Aaron sank into darkness, he smelled petrol in the air. The flicker of flame spread across the library floor toward the ancient books. What had he done?

CHAPTER 1

MORGAN SIERRA STOOD ON the edge of what remained of the still-smoldering library. The community gathered for Yom Kippur had stopped the fire from spreading too far, but much was burned and much more ruined by the water used to put it out.

Smoke rose from the pyre and ashes danced on the morning breeze, a bitter sight for Jews whose collective memory still echoed with the horrors of the Holocaust. The rise of the far-right in the rest of Europe seemed a long way from the open society of Amsterdam, but as she gazed into the embers, Morgan couldn't help but wonder whether racial hatred had driven this attack as it had so many times before — and surely would again.

She and Jake Timber had arrived an hour ago on a red-eye flight from London, swiftly organized when Director Marietti discovered the target of the fire. He hadn't said much on the phone, and his reticence was puzzling. ARKANE rarely became involved with hate crimes or terrorism of the everyday kind.

The Arcane Religious Knowledge And Numinous Experience (ARKANE) Institute investigated supernatural mysteries around the world. They focused on religious and occult forces, relics of power, and ancient places of blood rather than the more obvious terrestrial threats. Although the modern world might deny the existence of such things, Morgan had seen enough on her many missions to accept that not everything was as it seemed. Perhaps that was just as true today.

The wind changed direction and whipped the smoke around in a mini tornado. Morgan tasted ash in her mouth, the charred and bitter remains of the precious books of the library. The smell of mourning would linger in her clothes, a reminder of what had been lost.

On the flight over, she had read about the place in a hastily put together dossier from the archives of the ARKANE databases. Ets Haim was the oldest functioning Jewish library in the world, established by *conversos*, Jews forced to convert to Christianity who fled Portugal as the Inquisition scoured their ranks for souls to save and bodies to burn.

In 1492, the Jews of Spain had been expelled, and many retreated to Portugal, initially a safe haven of tolerance. But only a few years later, the Portuguese Jews were forced to convert in their turn. Some integrated into Christian society, but others fled to places where they could live in freedom, with some arriving in Amsterdam in the 1600s. Bet Jacob, the first Jewish community in Amsterdam, was formed in 1602 and the library started with its first Torah scroll.

Its literary prowess grew as the Dutch Republic became a center for printing and publishing in the seventeenth century. The 'bookshop of the world' used the distribution network of trade routes to ship books to all corners of the empire, and Amsterdam became one of Europe's leading hubs for Jewish printing.

Over the years, thousands of Portuguese and Spanish manuscripts found their way to Ets Haim, a trusted resting place for the written traditions of a persecuted people driven from their homes. The Netherlands had been a haven, but even this place had not escaped the Nazis, who murdered seventy-five percent of the Jewish population after the invasion. They came for the library in the summer of 1943; the books packed into crates and shipped to Germany, but the Allies recovered and returned them in 1946.

Lack of funds threatened the library once more in the 1970s, but finally, in 2003, the UNESCO Memory of the World Register added the collection in recognition of its universal value and documentary heritage. The Jewish Cultural Quarter now thrived in the modern city, tolerant of their faith once more, and the library now contained over 25,000 printed books and hundreds of manuscripts and other fragments.

Ets Haim also held rare Kabbalistic texts, and Morgan wondered whether her father had visited as part of his own study. He had been a scholar of the ancient Jewish mystical tradition, murdered for his knowledge as one of the Remnant and avenged at the Gates of Hell.

"Morgan!" Jake called from across the pyre, beckoning her over through the billowing smoke. He stood with an old Rabbi, the man's face creased with deep lines of wisdom etched by years of serving the Jewish community. But ash now smudged the lines, and exhaustion lay heavy on his shoulders.

Morgan walked around the edge of the pyre to join them. Jake's muscular frame looked even larger next to the diminutive Rabbi, and his usual dark stubble was more pronounced given their early start. A faint corkscrew scar twisted away from the corner of his left eyebrow, which only served to emphasize his amber-brown eyes. They reflected a keen interest right now, one that made Morgan draw closer with curiosity. She knew that look. Jake had discovered something that might explain why they were here.

"Rabbi Cohen, this is Morgan Sierra. We work together at ARKANE."

The Rabbi studied her more closely, his keen gaze

assessing the planes of her angular face. Morgan brushed her dark curls back reflexively under his scrutiny. She had inherited her father's Sephardic Jewish looks with the dark hair and tawny skin of Spanish heritage, although her eyes were unusual. A keen blue with a slash of violet in the right eye.

"Sierra?" the Rabbi said, his English slightly modulated with a Dutch accent. "We had a scholar here once with that name."

Morgan smiled. "The name is not so unusual, but my father, Leon Sierra, was indeed a Kabbalist scholar. It's possible he came to study here at your wonderful collection…" Her words trailed off and her smile faded as she realized that the books her father studied were most likely gone.

The Rabbi shook his head and sighed. "We know not the plans of God. Your father would have known that as well as I do." He pointed to the back of the pyre nearest the wall of the synagogue complex. "I was just telling Jake about a part of our collection that I fear may be responsible for this destruction."

He took a few steps forward until his shoes touched the edge of the smoldering pile, as if he would clamber over the ruins toward it. "We won't know for sure what's salvageable until the remains cool and we can dig underneath."

He turned to face them again. Morgan saw a fire in his eyes reflected from the embers and kindled by the determination that drove the Jews of Amsterdam to survive when they were hounded from their homes so many generations ago.

"The fire crew said that the epicenter was at the very back of the library, where they also found the burned corpse of one of our congregation. Aaron Heertje, one of my students." The Rabbi put a hand to his forehead and swayed a little.

Jake reached out to steady him, supporting his arm as the Rabbi continued. "The police informed us that the body of his wife, Rachel, was found at their home. They asked whether Aaron was depressed, whether perhaps this was a murder suicide, but I think it is far more, which is why I called Director Marietti. He and I have known each other for many years and he clearly trusts you in his stead." He stood tall again and took a deep breath. "Come, it will be easier to show you."

Rabbi Cohen shuffled toward the office complex on the opposite side of the courtyard, Morgan and Jake following close behind. The Rabbi pushed open the door and led them through to his office. It was a combination of ancient and modern with mahogany shelves laden with books, framed pictures from the history of the synagogue on the walls, and a wide desk inlaid with faded brown leather. A map of the world from the seventeenth century was mounted in an ornate frame marked with lines that snaked out from Portugal to the ends of the known world at the time.

The Rabbi opened a drawer and pulled out a slim laptop, its sleek modernity a sharp contrast to the timeworn surroundings.

He placed it on the desk and opened it up, then beckoned Morgan and Jake to gather closer. He tapped a few keys and pulled up a list of manuscripts and an index of the library. "We keep to the old traditions, but we also use technology to enhance our lives. The Lord gave us quick minds for a reason."

He clicked through to an image, a fragment of a map illustrated with looped vines with spiked leaves and crimson flowers in front of a spreading tree on the edge of a river. The vibrant colors were unusual in a tradition that studied the stark letters of the Hebrew alphabet shaped into the words of the divine, and Jewish scrolls rarely featured such images. There were symbols and words on the fragment, but it was clearly just a portion of the whole.

"Ets Haim," the Rabbi said, his voice wistful. "The Tree of

Life from the book of Genesis, chapter three, after which the library is named." He closed his eyes as he recited the verses in English. "'The man has now become like one of us, knowing good and evil. He must not be allowed to reach out his hand and take also from the tree of life and eat, and live forever. So the Lord God banished him from the Garden of Eden to work the ground from which he had been taken. After he drove the man out, he placed on the east side of the Garden of Eden cherubim and a flaming sword flashing back and forth to guard the way to the tree of life.'"

As he spoke the words, Morgan bent closer to examine the image. The sharp edges of the thorns looked menacing as if the vines were alive and could slash apart and devour whatever approached.

This was no gentle Eden.

The Rabbi opened his eyes once more. "Few knew of this fragment, but it was kept at the back of the library where the fire started. I didn't think Aaron knew of it, but perhaps he discovered its existence somehow."

"So what exactly is it?" Jake asked.

The Rabbi scrolled across the image to focus on the tree by the river, only partially visible before the torn edge. "This is part of a map that reveals the true location of the Garden of Eden, a place forbidden to us and a knowledge handed down to a select few over generations. It was torn into four pieces when the Portuguese betrayed the Jews and allowed the Inquisition to tear the community apart. One piece came here, but the others are scattered, I know not where. Perhaps someone is trying to put them together again."

Morgan looked over at Jake as he stood back to consider the Rabbi's words. His brow furrowed as he studied the image, and his dark eyes were contemplative. Perhaps in the past, they both would have been doubtful that such a thing was possible. But such wonders filled the vaults below the ARKANE headquarters in Trafalgar Square in London, and she had seen things that dissolved her own doubts over time. If this truly was part of a map to the Garden of Eden, if the Tree of Life was even a possibility, then she and Jake had to find it first.

The location of Eden was a powerful secret coveted by believers of Judaism, Islam and Christianity alike, three powerful religions that would use any means necessary to take control of such a place. But more than that, it was every ecological warrior's symbolic home, a place where Nature came first and humanity created as an afterthought.

Then there were those who pursued immortality at any price, the Silicon Valley billionaires who believed they could cheat death. She and Jake had encountered such people in the hunt for the Hand of Ezekiel — the bones that would raise the dead — and they had vast resources at their finger-tips. There were so many people who would seek the Garden of Eden if it truly was a place on Earth. It was hard to know where to start.

Morgan smiled to herself at the challenge ahead. In the last months since she and Jake had knelt together on the island of Alcatraz, she had immersed herself in the ARKANE archives during the day, researching and learning to increase her knowledge. By night, she had trained to her physical limits, sometimes alongside Jake in the state-of-the-art gym, but often separately with a Krav Maga coach to regain her former strength and skill in the Israeli martial art. The burns on her skin from the great serpent had faded now, and she had regained her focus. She was back in control and ready for the next mission.

Jake walked around the desk and stood before the map of the Portuguese Empire, tracing the lines with a fingertip. "The Jews of Portugal scattered all over the globe in the wake of persecution. How do we know where to start looking for the other fragments?"

The Rabbi pushed back his chair with a creak and shuffled

over. He reached up a finger and pointed to a city on the ocean. "You must start where it all began."

CHAPTER 2

Aurelia dos Santos Fidalgo stood on the edge of the vast open pit mine, its levels exposed as it descended deep into the earth. Copper-colored rock strata stretched as far as she could see, fading into the distance, and bleeding into the bright blue of the Brazilian sky above.

The giant trucks that transported ore to the processing area looked like toys from this distance high above, but the din of their engines echoed up the canyon regardless, the sound of weapons wielded daily against the land. The roads they traveled were scars that deepened every day, marks that Aurelia imagined were etched upon her own heart.

Mina de Fidalgo was her father's dream. Billions of tons of iron ore lay in the rock along with gold, manganese, bauxite, copper and nickel and he had spent his life creating this place. He fought hard for the permits to excavate this area of protected rainforest and once granted, he accelerated development. Each truck full of ore was another stack of dollars in his bank account, each gouge from the land lined his pockets and those of the corrupt government he propped up with his growing wealth. Now Aurelia stood in his bloated mansion on the edge of the mine.

The house had been constructed far away from the original dig, but over the years, the mine expanded until her father's grand dwelling sat right on the edge of the precipice. She put her hand against the glass window. Her brown skin looked almost translucent in the sunlight, and she spread out her thin fingers to try to blot out the wound on the land.

If only she could erase the whole thing.

But her father's recent death had not given her complete power over the mining company. It had only made her a figurehead with his name. The Board retained decision-making power, and they had plans to expand into the National Park on the western edge of the mine. It was nominally protected for biodiversity and conservation, but Aurelia knew it was only a matter of time before the company cut further into her beloved rainforest.

She turned from the window and sat down at the long tigerwood table carved from a single piece, its rich grain oiled and polished to a bright sheen. She wished it still grew in the forest, a living being, pulsing with sap, every ring a memoir of its long life. But her father had hacked it down himself and made the table back in the early days of his marriage when he dreamed of a vast family. He wanted strong sons to carry his name and beautiful daughters to marry off to wealthy landowners, an ever-expanding empire. This grand house had been but a dream back then, when the rainforest was thick and lush and his plans for the mine were just stakes in the ground.

The years passed and wealth flowed in abundance, but her father's goal of a huge family remained out of reach. Her mother miscarried over and over, her womb barren even as the ground gave up its lifeblood.

As her father told it, Aurelia was a child given by God as a reward for his years of dedicated service. But her mother had whispered the truth as she lay dying from lung cancer a few years back, the same disease that had carried off her father in recent months, both of them killed by toxic fumes from the very mine that had enriched them. The truth of her birth was a secret that could end Aurelia's position in the mining company, and she could not risk that until everything was in place.

A gentle knock at the door and the maid walked in with a breakfast tray. Her eyes remained lowered as she put it down at the only place setting and hurried out. Aurelia didn't know her name. She didn't know any of the local staff whose livelihood depended on the mine. There were thousands of people employed here — manual laborers, truck drivers, ore processors, scientists. The newly created wealth benefitted all levels of society — but at the expense of the land.

Aurelia didn't need to know their names because all of this would disappear soon enough. All these people would die, and her own time would inevitably come. One human life was a mere brief flicker of light against the dark expanse of the world. But some could flare brighter than others, and she intended to leave a legacy far greater than her father's.

She sat in the seat she had always taken in the family hierarchy. She could not bear to sit in her father's grand chair, and she would not take her mother's inferior position. Aurelia took a sip of green tea from a white porcelain cup, delicate crockery given to her mother back in the days when her father's wealth expanded and potential business partners came courting. Her mother had never liked the crockery or even much of her life out here, but she had done what she had to for her husband and eventually learned to tame her wilder nature. Aurelia had grown up here overlooking the mine, her mother's doted-on princess, her father's only child. The heir who would take over his empire when he died.

"This is all for you, *anjinha*," he would say. "Never forget it. This is your inheritance."

Even on his deathbed, her father still urged Aurelia on to greater things. But he had never noticed, or perhaps never cared, how she always gazed toward the rainforest instead of the mine.

Aurelia checked her breakfast plate carefully. Sometimes the maid put on too much, but today it was correct. Ten almonds. Ten small pieces of her favorite white melon, *melão branco*, cut into perfect squares. A tablespoonful of lentils.

She slowly picked up one almond, placed it in her mouth and forced herself to chew, wishing as she did every day that she didn't have to eat. Every calorie of energy she took from the world was one less for Nature's own survival. Her family had already taken so much from this land, and she hated to be the cause of yet more destruction. She closed her eyes and forced it down. It was important to sustain herself for the journey ahead, but perhaps it wouldn't be much longer. Perhaps this time they would find it.

Aurelia glanced at her phone, but the screen lay black and dormant. No word yet.

She picked up a square of melon and placed it on her tongue, letting sweetness flood her mouth. It was almost too much pleasure, and she longed to spit it out. She did not deserve such joy, but she had to eat. Her bones were brittle, her joints ached, and her skin lay tight against her frame. Whereas once she had been praised for her slim form, most would not even look at her now, crossing themselves as she passed as if to ward off the inevitable death that must come for all. But Aurelia didn't care for their opinion. She only had to sustain herself until she achieved her goal, and surely, it was closer now.

The cry of a harpy eagle came from outside, its wings outstretched as it soared on the hot air rising from the pit. Aurelia watched it with envy, wishing she could be as free. Did the eagle mourn the loss of its land as much as she did?

She speared another cube of melon and raised it to her lips, smelling the sweetness before taking a dainty bite. As she lifted the fork, the crockery vibrated on the table as the excavation below shook the foundations.

The Board wanted to excavate directly under the mansion,

to blow apart the rock beneath. In truth, Aurelia would be happy to see this place demolished, but she did everything in her power to thwart them, withholding permission for its removal claiming emotional distress at the thought of losing her family home. They said they would rebuild it exactly as she remembered, but miles away from the noise and dust so it would be even better. But Aurelia wanted to wake every day to the din of the mine, each clang a sound of the end of the world. For that is what it was.

They would never stop. These voracious men clawed at the ground and sold truckloads of it for gold. They raped and stabbed and slashed and burned the Earth that they had once seen as a mother, and yet still She lived.

Enough.

It was time to restore Nature to Her rightful place, and Aurelia intended to fulfill the promise of her birth.

On her deathbed, her mother had beckoned Aurelia over. Her skin clung tight to her skull, the flesh hollowed out by cancer. She could barely speak for coughing, but she persisted, whispering between labored breaths.

"The Earth Mother punished me for the sins of your father. His polluted seed would not grow in my womb and every child that began to grow died within me until blood ran freely once more." Her eyes filled with tears. "So many babies…"

She wiped the tears away as her gaze grew hard and determined. "After each time, he would return in the dark, force himself upon me even as the blood of the lost lay wet upon my skin. He would pray as he did it, asking God for a miracle to open my barren womb. But as the years went by and the wound in the ground grew deeper, I understood that the land scarred me within. The Earth Mother was raped as I was and She would never let me be fertile while Her body was broken apart."

She coughed slightly, and it turned into a hacking retch that convulsed her body.

Aurelia held honeyed water to her mother's cracked lips. "What then, *mãe*?"

Her mother took a deep breath and sighed. "I went to the only place I could turn to. The rainforest — and the shaman." She smiled, her eyes alive with memory. "I traveled the old ways, unknown to your father, so he could not follow or send a man to track me. My people — your people, Aurelia — are rainforest dwellers who thrive under the green canopy. My soul died a little every day I lived on the scar, but as I walked into the forest, the call of the howler monkeys nourished me. The smell of the damp earth and the bright flowers replenished me, and the nuts and berries I foraged on the way renewed my health. I found the village on the third day. The shaman sat by the remains of a fire, staring into the embers. He looked up with no surprise and nodded in welcome."

Her voice trailed off as she closed her eyes, her skin as pale as the waxy petals of an Amazon orchid.

Aurelia shook her a little, desperate to know the rest of the story, the truth of her history. "What happened then? How long did you stay?"

Her mother's eyes opened once more, the color deepening to the brown of Brazil nut wood with a hint of green, the colors of Nature restored once more.

"The shaman passed his gourd for me to drink and as night fell, the other villagers gathered around. Strong men with limbs like the trees, women at one with the rainforest. We sang songs of our ancestors under the full moon and welcomed the Goddess into our midst. I entered the upper realms that night and you were planted within me."

She grasped Aurelia's hand, her grip suddenly tight. "I know it, for when I woke the next morning, the shaman still sat by the fire. This time, he smiled at me before placing a hand on my belly."

Aurelia frowned. "So, who was my father?"

Her mother shook her head. "It doesn't matter whose seed you came from. You were born through me. You are a true child of the rainforest, a pure soul of the trees made flesh."

She pointed out the window toward the scar of the deep mine. "You were born to avenge the rainforest, but your father must never know of your lineage. I came out of the forest several weeks later and accepted his advances once more, but I knew you already grew within me. He considered you a miracle from his God, the one who teaches that man is the pinnacle of creation, but you truly are a child of Nature. When it is time, you must take your place and tear down all that he has built."

Her mother died later that day, and her father made sure she had a proper Catholic burial with all the trappings of the religion Aurelia knew her mother hated. But she smiled to herself as the casket passed by, for her mother was not in that hard wooden box. Her spirit soared high above, drifting back into the rainforest, part of the Earth once more.

Soon after, Aurelia told her father she was going to Rio de Janeiro, to take some time out to think about her life.

He had waved her away, his focus on the latest iron ore figures from the mine. "Go. Spend what you like. Have a good time." He looked up. "Find yourself a young man, have some fun."

But Aurelia had not traveled to the big city for nights of pleasurable excess. She had journeyed deep into the Amazon in search of her true ancestry. The village her mother spoke of had been moved on by deforestation, but deep in the green, she found a shaman willing to share the gourd with her. By his age, he might have been the man her mother sat with, but he did not remember such things.

In the depths of her trance, Aurelia saw what the world could become without humanity's pollution. An expanse of green with the flash of natural color from flowers and birds. Creatures living in harmony.

She would be the one to restore the Earth again.

After the rainforest, she had gone to Rio, but not to have fun. She spent months studying, learning, following a trail back to the European settlers of Brazil who wrote of a map to the Garden of Eden.

A sudden alarm sounded, interrupting her memories, the blaring din a warning of impending explosion.

Aurelia put her hands over her ears as the blast shook the house and echoed inside her head. Booming aftershocks rumbled through the ground, then the crash of rock collapsing, the roar of soil subsiding around it.

Another wound.

But this time, she relished the pain. It would be silenced soon enough.

At last, the noise subsided and there was a moment of silence before the giant trucks roared to life again. The manmade destruction would never stop unless she made it so.

Aurelia took a sip of her tea and separated the items on her plate. She would only eat half of each today. She trusted Mother Earth and it wouldn't be long until her body would return its energy to the rainforest where it belonged.

Her phone buzzed, and the screen lit up with a message from Amsterdam. The first piece was finally theirs.

Aurelia's father had spent his life exploiting and destroying the natural world. She would spend hers restoring Nature to Her rightful place.

CHAPTER 3

Belém, Lisbon, Portugal

SUNLIGHT DANCED ACROSS THE waters of the River Tagus, and the smell of salt came on the air from the Atlantic Ocean beyond. Morgan leaned back and closed her eyes for a moment, letting the balmy September sun warm her skin. It was only a short flight from Amsterdam, but Portugal felt like a different world. The culture was closer to her own Spanish heritage and the relaxed atmosphere of the beaches of Tel Aviv in Israel where she had grown up. Perhaps the sun melted away the sharp edges of the northern European personality here. She wished they had more time to get to know the place, but as ever, the mission marched on.

"I didn't know that the Portuguese once had such an empire," Jake said. He stood on the edge of a huge mosaic compass rose with a map of the world at its heart. Portuguese caravels roamed the marble oceans, ships in full sail marked with the red crosses of the Order of Christ. The date of discovery marked each significant port from the Cape of Good Hope on the Horn of Africa in 1488, to Goa, India in 1498 and on to Macau in the east in 1514. Traveling west, the Portuguese had reached Cananéia in 1502, claiming the land of Brazil for its empire.

"The Jews went with them," Morgan said. "Some in their new lives as *conversos*, New Christians, and others fleeing with ancient texts, holding to the faith of their ancestors."

She imagined the terror of heading out to sea on such a vast journey, afraid of what lay ahead but knowing that to leave was to live another day. Jews had found unexpected havens in the corners of the Portuguese Empire, but how were she and Jake to discover where to follow next?

"Impressive, isn't it?"

Morgan looked up to see a young woman standing astride the depiction of the Caribbean islands. She had a long, dark braid woven with colorful silk flowers and she held a cardboard tray with three takeaway coffee cups and a bulging paper bag.

"Director Marietti sent me to help while you're in Lisbon," she said. "I'm Ines, a student of archaeology on an ARKANE scholarship. He also mentioned that you might appreciate some of these." She raised the tray a little. "Coffee and the best *pastéis de nata* you'll find, possibly in the world."

Morgan strode across the mosaic of Latin America with enthusiasm. Black coffee was her one true addiction, and it was already turning out to be a long day.

"Thanks so much, Ines. You're a lifesaver." Morgan reached for the cup and took a sip.

Jake went for the pastries first, opening the paper bag with a crinkle. The smell of cinnamon and hot sugar wafted into the air as he pulled out a tiny, perfectly formed flaky pastry case with a deep yellow egg custard filling and cara-melized sugar on top. Most of it disappeared in one bite, and Morgan couldn't help but laugh at the pleasure on his face as Jake enjoyed the sweetness.

"Oh, these are good," he said, going in for another bite.

"Belém is the traditional home of the *pastel de nata*," Ines explained. "But they've spread all over the world now, and you can taste why."

Morgan turned to point at the huge Padrão dos Desco-brimentos, the Monument to the Discoveries, which rose high above them on the edge of the river. "Is that how they spread?"

Shaped like the prow of a caravel, the monument featured prominent Portuguese historical figures. Vasco da Gama, discoverer of the sea route to India; Ferdinand Magellan, first to circumnavigate the world; Pedro Álvares Cabral, discoverer of Brazil, and so many more, with Henry the Navigator at the prow looking out to sea. Every intricate carving had a distinct face, and each carried aspects of their lives — a sword, a cross, a manuscript, an astrolabe.

Ines led Morgan and Jake closer to the monument. "They carried our faith and our language — over 250 million people speak Portuguese around the world now — and you can even get an excellent *pastel de nata* in Macau."

She stared out across the water, her expression suddenly wistful. "We have a word in Portuguese, *saudade*, considered almost impossible to translate as it has no exact English equivalent. It is part longing and nostalgia, a kind of homesickness, and also conveys a sense of loss. Imagine a caravel leaving this port. One lover stands on the deck, the other on this shore. *Saudade* is the tension between the departed and the left behind."

"That's beautiful." Morgan looked up at the famous faces of the explorers. "It's incredible how far the Portuguese traveled. How does a nation go from ruling so much of the known world to being an almost forgotten corner of Europe?"

Ines shrugged. "I know, it's crazy. But every empire must fall. You live in England, so it must be the same there. A once great empire reduced to architecture, forgotten books, and memory."

Morgan nodded. "I think the English still have delusions of grandeur on the world stage, but you're right, empires must fall. The only question is how long they last and whether they realize they're at the end."

Jake gazed up at the figures. "And how many die at their hands," he whispered.

Ines turned back toward the road. "It wasn't just the far reaches of empire where my people slaughtered innocents. Come, I'll take you into the city and show you the archives."

She led them away from the busy tourist buses to a row of tuk-tuks, the three-wheeled auto-rickshaws used all over Asia but less common in Europe. Ines beckoned them over to one decorated with the same silk flowers she had wound in her plait.

"This is yours?" Morgan climbed into the tiny vehicle. Jake squeezed in next to her, his muscular frame pressing against her leg.

Ines patted the driver's seat proudly. "I used some of my grant money to buy it and I earn extra cash when I'm not busy at the archives. Tourists love the tuk-tuks. They're the fastest way to get around the city, that's for sure."

She pulled into the traffic and they sped off along the waterfront back toward the city. They passed through dilapidated areas with boarded up ruins and empty houses, as well as more industrial parts in what was still a busy port.

Morgan had second thoughts about Ines's seemingly gentle nature as she darted in and out of the traffic, turning around to point things out and weaving away from cars at the last moment with a liberal use of her blaring horn.

Jake grinned as they sped past a colorful food market. "This is awesome. Perhaps we could convince Marietti to get us one for the London office?"

They soon pulled up in the center of the old city and parked at the back of a rank of tuk-tuks. Ines went to speak with some other drivers, her lively chatter evidence of her place in the community.

She returned to them a minute later. "Come, it's this way."

They walked the last few streets along the distinctive pavements of the old city, *calçada portuguesa*, a unique style of hand-cut and hand-laid stone in wavy patterns of dark and white, as if the river twisted inland. Bright hand-painted *azulejos* tiles dotted the facades of houses and shops above, brought to Portugal by the Moors of North Africa.

Lisbon was truly an eclectic mix of cultures, modern evidence of the Portuguese Empire which brought immigrants from former colonies in Asia, Africa and Latin America. As they passed, the sound of *fado* drifted out of a bar, sometimes called the Portuguese blues for its blend of lyrical fatalism and resilience against the odds, a lament for an irrecoverable past.

They rounded a final corner and entered a tree-lined plaza where locals sat drinking coffee in dappled light next to the walls of the Convent of Our Lady of Carmel. Ines spoke to the clerk on the tourist desk and she waved them all inside.

They emerged into the medieval remains of a once grand house of worship. Morgan looked up in wonder at what remained of slender columns leading up to arches in the plain Gothic style. Somehow it seemed even more like a house of God without a roof, as the blue sky above formed the true vault of Heaven. Faith could never be contained in buildings constructed by human hands, and no matter the beauty of the place, Morgan always felt closer to the ineffable in nature than in man's creation. This ruined convent combined the best of both worlds.

"The 1755 earthquake destroyed this along with the great library," Ines explained. "The military used it for a while and eventually, it was partially reconstructed but then the 1969 earthquake damaged it further."

"Perhaps God prefers it this way," Morgan said softly.

Ines led them on through the nave toward the far end of the convent, which housed the small Archaeological Museum. She pushed open the door and led them through the chapel of the old apse, explaining interesting things as they walked. Pieces of sculpture retained from the ruins, Gothic sarcophagi including the tomb of King Ferdinand I from the fourteenth century, and even Bronze Age spears and tools.

Morgan recognized something of her younger self in Ines, the keen interest in so many areas and the difficulty of choosing an area to focus on. She had felt that way back in training for the Israel Defense Force, but her husband Elian's death in a hail of bullets on the Golan Heights had focused her search for meaning. She could only hope that Ines would not have to suffer such loss in order to find her true path.

"I've been working on a special project for ARKANE," the young woman explained. "There are manuscripts here that date back to the Catholic archives of the Portuguese Inquisition and even the Lisbon Massacre of 1506."

Jake frowned. "I always thought the Inquisition was Spanish?"

Morgan gave a rueful smile. "Fanaticism knows no borders."

Ines led them on into an unusual chamber. Wooden bookshelves densely packed with leather-bound volumes lined the high stone walls. An Egyptian mummy lay in a painted sarcophagus dated from the second century BCE. Two sixteenth-century Peruvian mummies sat entombed in glass cases, hunched over with bound legs and shrunken, leathery flesh. It was a macabre room of vellum, bone and parchment, a contrast to the sanctuary of stone outside in the fresh air.

The chamber grew dark as clouds passed over the sun beyond the windows, and Morgan shivered a little at the dead flesh before her. It was nothing like the mummy crypt in Palermo where she and Jake had sought the Devil's Bible, but somehow this place had a truly grim atmosphere.

Ines opened one of the glass-fronted bookshelves and pulled out a heavy tome. Jake helped her heft it onto the top of the Egyptian mummy case, and she opened it to a section on the Lisbon Massacre.

"I wanted you to see this. The words of a monk who witnessed hundreds of Jews tortured, beaten to death by the mob or burnt at the stake at Rossio Square, just down the road."

Morgan walked over to the bookcase and stared in at the volumes. The ashes of the pyre of the library in Amsterdam were nothing to the number of Jews burned here in Lisbon and those countless souls immolated all over Europe across the generations. Most knew of the Holocaust, but pogroms were common all over the continent as her people were blamed for everything from plague to economic ruin.

She took a deep breath and turned back as Jake bent over the manuscript to look more closely at a page displaying a hand-drawn map. The illustration was similar to the Portuguese Empire on the wall of the Rabbi's office.

"Many of the New Christians, or *conversos*, who survived left after the massacre," Ines explained. "Any remaining escaped when the Portuguese Inquisition was established thirty years later. Of course, its influence spread throughout the empire, but some Jews found a haven in the colonies."

"We're looking for pieces of a particular manuscript," Morgan said. "Why would this help?"

Ines pointed to the map. "Look closer."

Morgan walked to the other side of the sarcophagus and bent over the tome.

Jake leaned back a little to let her see and pointed to a tiny sketch next to a line of ships sailing away from the coast. "Look familiar to you?"

It was a tiny illustration made by the hand of someone with great skill depicting curled vines with sharp spikes and crimson flowers.

"The word next to it," Ines said softly. "*Hortus.*"

"The Latin word for garden," Morgan finished for her as

she looked down at the caravels sailing east. "Then we will follow the same path."

They walked back outside together and as a taxi pulled up, Morgan smiled at Ines. "Come to the London ARKANE office sometime. I'd love to show you what we have in our archives. I think you would find it fascinating."

Ines beamed with enthusiasm. "I'd love that, thank you. I'll put a request in after the summer break."

*   *   *

Frik Versfeld pulled his baseball cap lower over his forehead, his eyes hidden from view by designer mirrored sunglasses as he gazed at the man who stood only meters away outside the convent walls. It took everything he had to rein in the anger that surged inside as he focused on the man's features.

It had to be him. Jake Timber.

Frik raised a hand to touch his throat, fingertips brushing the ugly scars that still marred his body even after countless grafts and surgery. He was a monster because of what Jake had done years ago and he had dreamed of revenge for so long, but Jake had disappeared off grid. What was he doing here now?

Frik raised his phone and took several photos of the convent walls, as any tourist might do, but he made sure to get Jake and the two women with him in the frame.

As Jake stepped into a taxi with the older woman, Frik followed the younger one as she walked away. His fingers itched to wrap around her slim neck. She would tell him what they had found within the convent and where Jake would go next. Aurelia had ordered him to find the Jewish archive in Lisbon as a way forward in their search for the map to Eden, but now, it seemed, he might be able to settle a more personal score along the way.

CHAPTER 4

Every step he took in this sacred place was one step closer to Heaven. Guram gritted his teeth against the pain as the burning coals seared the flesh on the bottom of his feet, and he forced himself not to run. The way of the Ignis Flammae was the path of flame, and if he could not bear this temporal agony, how could he ever expect to fight for the cause against the forces of ever-growing darkness in the world above.

The smell of burning flesh wafted through the air, tainting the incense that rose in eddies around the Brothers. They lined the edge of the trench of hot coals and chanted the words of the prophet Isaiah, chapter 43.

"Ambulaveris in igne non conbureris et flamma non ardebit. When you walk through the fire, you will not be burned; the flames will not set you ablaze."

Guram repeated the familiar words along with them and slowed his steps. His reward would be greater the more he demonstrated his faith.

Each of the Brothers wore a forest green robe woven through with thorns to remind them of the violence of Nature, each movement bringing a prick, a cut, a slice of pain so they would never forget the true nature of Eden. Five men were chosen from each generation to become Warriors of the Ignis Flammae, to carry one of the flaming swords after which they were named. There were other lay Brothers out in the cities, those who lived closer to the Worldly so they might see yet not be seen, and shape those unknowing by means of enterprise, but Guram's destiny was amongst the Warriors.

He fixed his gaze on the Abbot at the end of the burning trench and took another step. The old man was shrunken in stature, but his aged body still stood upright and strong. None of the Brothers would dare challenge him in combat, and he still joined them in training, wielding his own sword with deadly skill. He held that weapon in front of him now, the blade alive with blue fire.

If Guram could reach it and grasp the burning weapon, the Brotherhood would welcome him. He gulped down his pain and took one more step. The brief moment his foot was aloft allowed a whisper of cool air to touch the blistered skin. He wanted to howl, to scream, to run from this place and soothe his agony, but he had come so far. This was the final stage, the last few moments before his life of service truly began.

He gazed beyond the Abbot to the ancient door carved with hooked vines and voracious flowers. If he could make it to the end, he would finally see the Garden. The pain would be worth it. Guram bit down hard on his lip and looked again at the Abbot, the man's dark eyes reflecting the flames from the sword. He took another step.

The Abbot was Yazidi just as Guram was, although many races were represented amongst the Brothers. Men of faith from throughout the known world called to fight against the insatiable appetite of Nature. Guram felt a kinship with the old man, an understanding of persecution and what it took to survive.

The Yazidis had faced extinction many times over millennia, an ancient race that dwelled in what was once Mesopotamia, now the disputed territories of Northern Iraq. Their belief system was ancient, one God who had entrusted the care of the world to seven holy beings, with the Peacock Angel their most precious. But Guram found that the mission to protect Eden transcended the faith of his people, and even though he still carried a peacock's feather, he would lay it down to take up the flaming sword.

The Catholic Church had disavowed the Order of the Ignis Flammae early in the Reformation period, as Europe emerged from the darkness of the Middle Ages. The Pope and his well-meaning Cardinals had disbanded the Ignis Flammae, commanding them to join other Orders, preferring to believe that Eden was no longer a threat, and the Garden faded into history. But the Ignis Flammae knew the truth. They had gone underground, the monks more aware than ever of the danger that humanity faced from Mother Nature, the sworn enemy of civilization.

The chanting of the Brothers rose in volume as Guram reached the end of the burning channel and stood before the Abbot. The old man stared down at him, a challenge in his eyes. If there was any sign of weakness, of desperation to escape the burning torture, Guram would be cast out. He had seen many novices leave here broken in body and spirit when they failed the test of fire. But he would not falter.

He stood his ground, his feet searing on the coals, pain lancing up his legs. He stared up into the Abbot's eyes, biting his lip again until the metallic taste of blood flooded his mouth.

A few more seconds.

Just when the screaming in Guram's head reached a crescendo, the Abbot thrust the flaming sword out in front of him. "Take it, Brother. Step into your new life."

Blue flames licked the folded steel, the mottled effect like ripples on the surface of a deep pool. The sharp blade reflected the hooded Brothers around him and Guram could see his own face there too, his brown skin covered in sweat and his crooked nose, broken in an Iraqi dungeon. But there was a new pride in his eyes as he reached for the blade with his left hand.

His fingers closed around the sword and he let the flame lick his skin. The hot metal cut into his palm and blood bubbled up around the wound.

The Abbot nodded and reached for his other hand. "Rise, Brother. You are now a Warrior of the Ignis Flammae. Welcome to the Garden."

The Brothers rushed forward and pulled Guram from the fiery pit. He tumbled into their arms, blinking back tears — not from the pain, but from a sense of being uplifted, finally blessed and accepted into this holy place.

The Abbot knelt by him as the Brothers tended to his wounds. "Let us heal you, my son."

One monk applied a cool balm and fresh bandages around Guram's burned feet, another dabbed salve on his palm and wrapped it with linen. The Abbot himself lifted a cup to Guram's lips. "Drink this down. The Garden's poison can also be its cure."

Guram took a sip and almost gagged on the bitter juice, but as it trickled down his throat, a fire ignited inside. He gulped it down and his pain melted away even as the cavern grew hazy around him and his mind lifted away from his wounded body. Smoke from the fire merged with incense and whirled into shapes of skeletal figures, dead Brothers come to honor the new member of their ranks. He nodded to them and they parted before the ancient wooden door.

Its carvings writhed and looping vines with hooked claws squirmed over the wood, as if to escape their prison. The flowers bloomed into gaping maws, sharp spines emerging like tiny teeth ready to shred any prey that came near.

The Abbot bent close. "You see it, don't you, Brother. The truth of the Garden is right there on the door, but only the chosen see Eden as She really is. The most dangerous foe mankind can ever face, never resting in Her desire to take back the land that once belonged only to Nature. We perish and die in ever greater numbers to hold Her back and yet our blood only nourishes and strengthens Her."

He reached inside his robes to grasp a silver pendant that hung around his neck. He tightened his fist around it as if gaining strength from the metal talisman. He sighed before speaking once more. "The Lord placed an angel with a flaming sword east of Eden to stop mankind finding it again. We are the last in that line of defense. Now you are one of us, it is time for you to see what we protect the world from."

The Abbot stood and beckoned two of the Brothers over. They laid a woven green blanket on the ground and helped Guram onto it, then lifted him as if in a cradle. The Abbot slowly walked to the ancient door, his footsteps slowing as he approached as if a great weight settled over him.

When they reached the door, he turned to face the Brothers. "Hide your eyes, lest you be taken in by Her treachery."

The two Brothers laid Guram down and pulled green rags from their robes, tying them around their heads so they could no longer see. Guram's heart beat faster as he considered what might lie behind the door. What could be so terrifying that Brothers who had been inside themselves must not witness what lay beyond?

The Abbot faced the door once again and turned the huge key in its ancient lock. A click and it swung open with ease. The smell of wet earth and pungent flowers wafted from inside. It was dark at first, but the light from the fire pit cast a beam that illuminated the thick trunk of a gigantic tree in the depths of the Garden.

A writhing vine shot out the door and wrapped itself around the Abbot's foot.

He slashed down with his flaming sword and the plant jerked back inside, leaving a piece of itself on the stone. The Abbot crushed it with his heel, grinding it to a pulp, his face contorted with hatred.

"Now we go in, Brother, and I will stand beside you as you face Her."

The Abbot walked inside, his flaming sword held high as

he advanced. The two blindfolded Brothers picked up the blanket again and walked after him. Guram clutched the edge of the material, his knuckles white with terror as they entered the Garden, blood seeping from his wounds as he readied himself to face what lay ahead.

The Brothers placed Guram on a patch of earth and retreated out of the door quickly, closing it behind them. The click of the key resounded ominously in the cave, and terror rose in Guram's chest at the thought of being trapped here.

The Abbot stood next to him, flaming sword held high, eyes fixed on the darkness beyond. "Whatever you see, Brother, hold steady."

His voice wavered as if they faced some terrifying foe, but only the gentle sound of rain came from further back in the cave, a peaceful note of water refreshing the soil. Guram remembered sitting with his mother on their verandah during monsoon season, watching raindrops ripple in the puddles, listening to her prayers of thanks to God for sending much-needed water. The memory filled him with a calm peace, and he wondered how the Garden could be considered so terrifying.

He turned his face up to the roof, seeking drops of rain to cool his burned skin, but nothing came except the sound in the distance and the smell of damp earth.

A tendril of vine slowly emerged beside him, a tiny green shoot, a symbol of hope in every culture. Guram watched as it pushed out of the ground and fragmented the surface of the soil. It seemed harmless, perfect in its creation. He frowned in confusion. Was the Garden actually a sanctuary?

The sound of rain intensified.

Guram glanced up. The Abbot clutched his flaming sword more tightly as he stood in a fighting stance and faced the darkness beyond.

A roll of thunder and then a flash of lightning illuminated

the cave. Guram gasped to see its true expanse, an underground rainforest with green of every shade and flowers of every hue. A gigantic tree rose in the center, its branches spreading out like the heavens, and somehow, it maintained its own weather system deep underground.

He felt a tightening around his wrists and looked down to see the tiny vine was now as thick as his palm was wide. It wrapped around his limbs and pulled him tight against the earth, oozing poisonous sap onto his skin.

"Help!" Guram screamed, but the Abbot could only slash at the ferocious vines attacking his own legs, the fire of his sword fading as the heavy rain reached them and hammered down from above.

The Abbot fell to the ground as the vines wound up his frame faster than he could cut them away. The rain soon extinguished the fire on his sword and they lay at the mercy of the Garden.

The storm descended with fury, and Guram could only surrender to the cacophony. In the howling of the wind and the hammering of the rain, he heard the agony of those drowned in Her floods and ocean rage, whose bodies were smashed apart by tornadoes or crushed by earthquakes, who convulsed as they ate Her poisonous plants. He listened as She burned humanity in wild fires and volcanic ash and even with the rays of the blistering sun. She released noxious fumes to suffocate Her enemies, plagues to decimate the population, and starved the rest when She withheld her bounty. Ultimately, She consumed their flesh and bones, devouring life and using it to grow more of Herself. Guram screamed as the truth of the Garden was revealed to his fragmented mind, and he wept at the futility of fighting such a powerful foe.

The pungent stench of rotting vegetation filled his senses as a gigantic corpse flower descended, its petals unfurling as it sank its hood over his face. Maggots erupted from the earth, their squirming white bodies surging over Guram's skin. Their tiny mouths latched onto his skin as the blind creatures tried to burrow into his flesh.

He flailed under the lattice of vines, desperately trying to escape his bonds, sobbing and screaming even as thick green stems forced their way into his mouth. They silenced him as they twisted down his throat, choking and strangling as they overcame his final ounce of strength. The vines began to drag his body toward the great Tree.

As Guram's vision faded to black, the ancient door burst open, and the Brotherhood stormed in, swords aflame. As he sank into darkness, he knew that he would do anything to stop Nature from taking back the world She once ruled.

* * *

Guram woke in the infirmary to the smell of fresh coffee, clean sheets and the antiseptic sting of dressings on his many wounds. Every inch of his body ached, but he sighed in pleasure at being back in civilization once more. He thanked the Lord that Nature was tamed and controlled within the walls of the monastery. The cave below the ground seemed but a nightmare, amplified by his drugged state after the trial by fire. Yet he couldn't deny the proof on his skin, the raised welts around his wrists from the poisonous vines, the ache in his throat from the violation of its thorny stems.

The Abbot came into the room and limped over slowly, every step clearly an effort. He sat on the side of the bed, his face gaunt, his flesh covered with tiny cuts.

"You did well, my son. You faced Her, and emerged with knowledge that few possess. Only Warriors may enter the Garden, and most in the Order do not even know the location of the sanctuary."

He reached for Guram's sword hand and took it in his

gnarled palm. "We are all in danger in these modern times. I fear discovery of the Garden and the release of Her power by those who don't understand what it means." He shook his head. "But I cannot face Her again. She grows stronger, and those who seek Her out will release Her power into the world if they can."

The Abbot clutched at the silver pendant around his neck. "The Tree of Life was never meant for us, as the Lord Himself said in Genesis. We were expelled from the Garden for our own good." His piercing gaze looked deep into Guram's soul. "Recover quickly, my son, then ready yourself to go into the world and stop those who seek to restore Eden."

CHAPTER 5

MORGAN BREATHED IN THE tropical air of Macau, an island city in the Pearl River Delta across the bay from Hong Kong and Shenzhen, a region of China that had expanded rapidly in the last decade of staggering economic growth.

It was good to be out in the open air after fifteen hours flying on a cargo plane. She had slept easily, a trick picked up during her years in the Israel Defense Force, but Morgan was grateful that the journey was quicker than the many months of open sea that the Portuguese traders would have faced.

Portugal had leased Macau for hundreds of years, establishing it as a trading post in 1557 before finally transferring it back to China in 1999 when it became a Special Administrative Region. Gambling was forbidden on the mainland but encouraged on Macau so the island became a resort destination, the Las Vegas of the East, every square inch packed with elaborate hotels offering every kind of hedonistic pleasure.

As they walked out of the terminal, Morgan's phone rang. Director Marietti's name came up on the screen and she answered right away, putting him on speaker so Jake could hear too.

"I have bad news," Marietti said, his tone somber. "Ines is dead. She was tortured and murdered, her neck burned to the bone with a lump of coal. One of our Portuguese agents found her just a few hours ago when she didn't turn up for a meeting."

Morgan could hardly breathe as his words echoed in her mind. The thought of the lively young woman with flowers in her braid suffering and dying because of their visit to Lisbon was too much. Even though they had met only briefly, she had seen so much of her own youthful optimism in Ines. Morgan thought of Father Ben and how he too had died because of an ARKANE mission. How many lives must they lose? Was it all worth the cost?

She handed the phone to Jake and walked away, leaving him to find out any other details.

Morgan looked out to sea and brushed a tear from her cheek, feeling the sting of cool air on her skin. A sensation that Ines would never experience again. She clenched her fists. She would find whoever was responsible and she would finish them.

A gentle touch on her shoulder. "Are you OK?"

Morgan turned and leaned into Jake's arms. He embraced her, and she buried her head against his muscled chest. He smelled of shaded pine forests, and his heartbeat was strong and regular. Morgan allowed the sound to anchor her and after a moment, she drew back.

His gaze was concerned, but they both knew each other so well now, there was no need to talk. Jake knew intimately of loss, and Morgan knew that he still grieved for Naomi Locasto, in particular, the agent lost in their last mission. But they both believed in something more than this physical world, although perhaps neither of them really knew what that meant. She hoped they would be together until at least one of them figured it out.

Morgan took a deep breath and let it out slowly. "We'll honor Ines by finding the fragments of the map."

Jake nodded, the muscles around his jaw tight with tension. "And whoever was responsible."

They walked to the gate and jumped in a taxi for the historic district.

Morgan gazed out the window as they drove from the airport, every block revealing another surprise. Ostentatious wealth in the supercars that whizzed past. Futurist extravagant architecture of hotels like the Morpheus in the City of Dreams, designed by architect Zaha Hadid. The metallic multi-hued blocks of the MGM Cotai reflecting the early morning light, their Chinese jewelry box aesthetic blending the ancient and modern. They passed the Eiffel Tower, half the height of the Parisian original and built to withstand a typhoon, certainly more impressive than the Las Vegas copy.

Much of this land had been reclaimed from the sea, drained and built upon, creating space for consumption and expansion at the expense of the natural environment. But beneath the affluence, there were clues to the hidden side of Macau, those who lived in poverty and spent their lives servicing the rich.

An older woman in a hotel uniform sat by the side of the road, oblivious to the traffic. She rested her head in her hands and her shoulders shook as if she sobbed. Morgan glimpsed a life lived on a knife-edge, perhaps the end of a job that was her only income, or grief for a life ended. Another person chewed up by the voracious city as it serviced those who could afford luxury but cast out the poor.

"Welcome to the historic center," the taxi driver said as he pulled up near the Ruins of St Paul's. The stacked arches loomed above them, the facade of what was originally the Church of Mater Dei and St Paul's College, the first western-style university in the Far East. Built of granite in the early 1600s in a Baroque style, most of it had been destroyed by fire in 1835.

Morgan paid for the taxi as Jake stretched his legs. As she turned to join him on the edge of the plaza, he spotted a pastry shop.

"Oh yes." Jake grinned. "I'm having some of those."

He jogged over and bought a bag of three *pastéis de nata*

then sauntered back over, delving into the bag to pop a whole one into his mouth. Morgan couldn't help but laugh as his cheeks bulged, and he swallowed the sweet pastry down. She pulled another out of the bag before he could finish them all and took a bite, allowing the delicious flavor to rejuvenate her after the long trip. Not quite as good as Belém, but tasty enough.

Morgan looked up at the facade in front of them. At first glance, it was a Christian monument with Mater Dei, Mother of God, inscribed upon the lintel, bronze statues of the Jesuit saints and the Virgin Mary in alcoves, and Jesus with a dove, representing the Holy Spirit. But the mix of cultures made this monument starkly different to anything Morgan had seen before in ecclesiastical architecture. Seven-headed dragons danced amongst the angels next to Portuguese merchant ships. Chinese characters engraved in stone pronounced 'Holy Mother tramples the heads of the dragon.' A peony representing China and a chrysanthemum representing Japan completed the frieze, the latter symbol from the Japanese Christian exiles who worked on the church in the early 1600s.

Jake pointed at the center of the third tier of columns. "Is that what I think it is?"

To the right of the Virgin Mary was what looked like a Tree of Life, its roots delving down into stone, its branches neatly pruned, its wildness tamed into allegory.

Morgan squinted up. It seemed too much of a coincidence, but yet, it was really there, carved by the faithful hundreds of years ago. History never ended, and symbols persisted through the ages, pointing the way to those who could read the signs.

"You're right, it's definitely a tree. We must be on the right track." She pulled out her phone and retrieved the information that Martin Klein, ARKANE's archivist, had sent on their way over. "Three hundred *converso* families settled here in the first wave of immigration and in 1579, the Jesuit Francisco de Meneses wrote of the existence of a Jewish community."

Jake frowned. "The Jesuits didn't have a great reputation for dealing with Jews."

Morgan shook her head. "No, but the closest inquisitors were in Goa, India, and it seems that this community managed to survive. In 1842, when Hong Kong was ceded to Great Britain, they moved over there and the first synagogue was established in 1857. But it's far more likely that any manuscripts were retrieved by the Jesuits and held in their library. It's not far from here."

They walked away from St Paul's along the pedestrianized streets toward the Church of St Dominic. Morgan found herself fascinated by the cultural mix of the city. This part of the historic district had clear signs of its colonial past, now enshrined as a UNESCO World Heritage Site. Signs were trilingual, with directions in English, Portuguese and Cantonese. There were even some traditional Portuguese *azulejos*, colorful ceramic tiles, along the side of government buildings. But it was also totally Asian, with Chinese lanterns hung above the pavements, the smell of delicious spicy Macanese food, and the sound of Chinese spoken by most of the surrounding tourists along with the blare of horns from the busy traffic.

The nearby sixteenth-century Church of St Dominic sat on the edge of a plaza paved with the traditional hand-cut Portuguese stone in waves of black and white, the *calçada portuguesa*. The church had three tiers in an elaborate Baroque style, painted in shades of ivory and mustard yellow with forest green shutters and doors.

Morgan and Jake walked inside and up into the bell tower, which now held the Museum of Sacred Art. It was a relatively small collection, arranged in groups of sacramental objects. Religious statues, chalices for Mass, liturgical vestments, and two large bells.

Morgan frowned. "This is nothing special. We need to find the library or somewhere the Jesuits might have kept their manuscripts."

Jake waved her over to one cabinet. "Wait a minute, check this out."

Morgan walked closer to the glass case. There was a piece of a manuscript inside, similar to the image the Rabbi had shown them in Amsterdam, with part of a tree in hues of brown and green, a blue river and words etched in Hebrew and Portuguese.

They had found the second fragment.

* * *

Frik remained in the shadow of a palm tree on the edge of the plaza as Jake and the woman he now knew as Morgan Sierra disappeared into the darkness of the church. The Fidalgo wealth and contacts had bought him a private jet to Macau, and he had arrived a few hours before the ARKANE agents on their cargo flight.

He had used the journey to fill in his knowledge with what he could find about the secretive agency and their public face in archaeological research and religious heritage. He had learned much from the young woman, Ines, before forcing that final burning coal through her neck. Frik smiled to himself as he remembered those last moments, the smell of smoke as it rose from her charred skin, her final breath choked into silence. It wouldn't be long until he watched Jake Timber die the same way.

Frik strode across the plaza toward the door of the church, clenching his fists as he readied himself for the confrontation he had dreamed of for so many years. As he reached the door, he typed a short code into his phone and began the countdown in his head.

*   *   *

Jake bent to the glass to examine the piece more closely. It certainly looked like part of the Tree of Life, but it still made little sense as a map. They would need help to figure out what it meant and whether it led to an actual physical location.

His own faith was rooted in the Christian tradition with the Bible as the literal word of God. But violence had shaken Jake's belief after the massacre of his family in a drug-fueled frenzy by a gang in Walkerville near Johannesburg. He had spent years in the military as part of the struggles of the nations of Africa to escape their colonial past, but also to free themselves from internal rivalry, tribal allegiances and corruption.

As a white South African, Jake understood the struggle of race. The color of his skin made many people dismiss his love of Africa. Yet his blood ran with the dust of the Great Karoo and the salt of the Cape, his lungs took their first breath in the rarefied air of the Drakensberg and he only felt truly at home when he touched the soil of his great continent.

As Morgan leaned in closer to examine the fragment, he smelled the coconut scent of her shampoo and part of him longed to brush the curls from the nape of her neck. They were both a mixture of cultures, a blend of the religious and historical choices that their ancestors had made and still echoed down the generations. Perhaps that's why they both felt at home within ARKANE's view of the world, where reality and the supernatural collided.

A deep boom roared up from outside.

The church shuddered.

The glass windows exploded inward with the force of the blast.

Jake reached for Morgan as they both leaped away from the hail of shards, pulling her into his arms as they tumbled to the floor. Glass rained down around them and Jake took most of it on his back, his jacket shielding them both.

A brief silence, then screams and the sound of sirens from outside.

"What the hell?" Morgan scrambled up and shook herself free of broken glass.

"We need to get out of here." Jake was on full alert now. The display case had shattered in the explosion and he reached in for the Eden fragment, tucking it inside his jacket pocket.

BOOM.

The explosion came from directly below this time. A blast of hot air beneath their feet. The billowing of fire igniting.

The old wooden floor cracked and crumbled into burning timber. Morgan tumbled into the flames.

CHAPTER 6

"No!" Jake reached out, his fingertips brushing hers as Morgan fell, disappearing into the billowing smoke.

A crash from below. A crack of burning timbers.

The floor beneath him crumbled in its turn, and Jake plummeted down after her.

He had learned to fall at an early age and relaxed his body, bending his limbs and tucking chin to chest as he plunged down into the fiery church.

The impact was hard and sharp against his ribs. Jake fell on his side onto an old wooden pew and rolled off into the embers of the burning floor, breath knocked from his lungs. Thick smoke rose up around him. He coughed, desperately trying to draw breath.

Jake couldn't see Morgan, couldn't hear anything but the roar of the voracious blaze as it devoured the ancient wooden church. He rolled to one side and gathered his strength, trying to push himself up as pain flared in his side.

An enormous man strode out of the smoke.

A figure of nightmare, his neck burned into layers of scars and puckered skin, his features twisted with hate. He wore a heavy leather jacket and fireproof gloves, clearly prepared for the blaze. Embers whirled around him as he took two quick steps forward and kicked Jake hard in his damaged ribs with a steel-toe-capped boot.

Jake saw it coming and tensed his stomach muscles, curling into the kick to absorb the blow. But it wasn't enough.

It knocked the remaining breath from his aching lungs and left him gasping as pain ricocheted through his body.

He tried to get up.

Another kick, harder his time. Jake couldn't help but moan with the pain.

"Stay down, Timber."

The man knew his name. How was that possible?

The scarred man reached down and pulled Jake's jacket open, tugging the fragment from his pocket. Flames roared around them, but the man showed no sense of urgency. He folded it carefully inside a metal tin and placed it inside his jacket. Then he picked up a piece of burning pew, a heavy chunk of wood, its end a glowing crimson.

Jake struggled to pull himself away, still gasping for breath.

The man stepped astride him, gaze fixed on his prey, the flaming wood held in one hand. He grinned and dropped his weight down onto Jake's chest, his knees pinning either arm.

"You don't remember me, do you?"

Jake shook his head, barely able to breathe with the weight on his chest, and the intense smoke.

The man brought the burning wood close to Jake's exposed throat. He leaned down, his voice barely audible over the crackle of flames. His eyes were the hard grey of flint, the color of stone mined from the deep earth.

A flash of memory and Jake suddenly recognized him. Frik Versfeld. A man he thought long dead after a mining accident in South Africa.

Frik smiled as recognition dawned in Jake's eyes. "You'll pay for what you did to me and my men that day, although your burning flesh won't smell as sweet as that pretty girl in Lisbon. You're responsible for her death, too."

Jake writhed and bucked his hips, trying to throw Frik off, but the man was huge, his weight immovable.

Frik grabbed a handful of Jake's hair and tugged his head back to expose his throat. He thrust the burning wood close to Jake's neck in the place where his own scars ravaged the skin.

Jake could feel the heat of it, smell Frik's sweat and the burning church, and hear blood pounding in his head as the brand came closer. The burning end touched his skin, almost a caress, then the pain intensified, scorching, blistering —

A heavy bronze candlestick swung out of the billowing smoke behind Frik, smashing against the side of his head, knocking him sideways.

As his weight shifted, Jake bucked his hips again, throwing his attacker off. Morgan stepped out of the conflagration, swinging the candlestick in her hands. Frik collapsed on the ground under a burning pew, ash and embers rising up as smoke swirled around his prone body.

Morgan leaned down to help Jake up as the sound of sirens came from outside. "Let's get out of here."

Jake scrambled to his feet, every movement sending a shard of pain through his body. "We need… to… deal with him."

He turned to point to Frik, but the body was gone. The man had dragged himself away in the fiery church — along with the map fragment.

Morgan and Jake stumbled outside. The fire brigade unrolled their hoses and soaked the church, evacuating the area and holding people back from the flames. Paramedics ran to the emerging survivors and helped them to an ambulance. As Jake sucked in oxygen and a medic tended to his burns, he drifted off into memory.

It was the summer after his parents and sister had been murdered.

The only way Jake could deal with their deaths was to join the military, but he had a few months before the next intake, so he took a job at one of the remote coal mines in South

Africa as a security guard. The punishing heat, long hours and dangerous work meant that he fell into an exhausted, dreamless sleep every night, thoughts of his family's butchered bodies kept at bay by extreme fatigue.

The camaraderie amongst the men helped too, a tough masculinity that allowed for no emotional breakdown, no sense of vulnerability, no chink of weakness. Jake was in peak physical condition that year, eating only to fuel his muscles, and in the hours he was off duty, he worked out at the gym on the edge of the veld, punishing his body into submission.

Other men joined him during those sessions, their grunts and heavy exhalation punctuating the sounds of the mine site. Frik Versfeld was one of them. He had been at the mine for a year already when Jake arrived, and initially he had been friendly enough. But when Jake was promoted to run the team, Frik undermined him. In subtle ways at first, waiting a beat too long before following an order, then spreading rumors about Jake's inability to make decisions.

But when someone sabotaged the workout equipment and a heavy weight almost crushed Jake's foot, he knew he had to have it out with Frik.

The confrontation was loud and almost came to blows, but Jake clenched his fists and let the other man vent, before he ordered Frik to take his security team to the deepest part of the mine for an inspection.

It was routine; it had to be done, but not on that day.

It could have been left until the weather was cooler, when tempers were not so frayed. But truth be told, Jake wanted Frik and his men out of the way.

They went to the bottom of the mine; they did their job, but while they were down there, a coal seam ignited.

The fire spread quickly. The alarm rang out and the mine site activated emergency protocols. They fought back the flames and reached Frik's team, pulling them back to the surface — but of the four who went down, only two were alive when they reached the hospital, both badly burned, both expected to die. One of those was Frik.

Jake was cleared of responsibility but he still resigned his position, throwing himself into the military, salving his conscience with dangerous missions until he met Elias Marietti that fateful night in the Sudan and joined ARKANE.

Since then, Jake had taken lives and seen many others die. He had also saved thousands of people and possibly altered the fate of humanity for the better with the recovery of powerful artifacts that could have been used for destruction. He had not thought of Frik or the mine in years — but now, a personal agenda threatened the mission.

Jake thought of Ines. Was he responsible for her fate or would Frik have taken her life, regardless? And if he sought the other fragments, who did he work for? Frik Versfeld was not a man of deep faith or deep pockets. He had to be hired muscle for someone else. Jake also had no doubt that Frik was behind the fire at Ets Haim, which meant that now, whoever they were, they had two pieces of the map.

Morgan put a hand on Jake's arm and pulled off her oxygen mask with the other. "Are you OK? You look more than just dazed. Should the paramedics check you for concussion?"

Ash smeared her features and highlighted the angles of her face. Dark curls hung loose from her ponytail, the ends singed, her clothes were disheveled and smelled of smoke. But despite her own condition, Morgan's blue eyes were alive with concern, the slash of violet in the right one even more vivid against the dark smudges on her skin.

Jake wanted to reach out and brush the ash gently from her cheek, but instead, he took a deep breath. While the oxygen refreshed his mind, the expansion of his lungs pushed against his damaged rib cage.

He assessed the level of pain against years of experience

with injury. "I think the bastard might have fractured my rib, but hopefully it's just bruised." He took another deep breath of the oxygen. "I know that man. He worked for me in a mine in South Africa. There was an accident…"

His words trailed off. The fire had been an accident and he could never have controlled its path, but he had sent Frik and the other men down there for no good reason that day. Jake's anger and frustration and inability to manage the situation had caused the death of two men and the brutalizing of another, who had now become a dangerous foe.

He breathed in once more and slowly exhaled, relishing the pain in his ribs. He deserved it, and he welcomed it. Pain meant that he was still alive, and whatever their past entanglement, he would not let Frik derail this mission. In fact, the man may have helped them by revealing himself.

He pulled up his mask. "Tell Martin to look into Frik Versfeld." He spelled it out for Morgan as she tapped into her phone, sending the message back to Martin Klein, the head archivist back at ARKANE headquarters.

Martin's nickname was Spooky because of his uncanny ability to discover obscure secrets within the interlinked databases he had constructed from accessing the world's knowledge — sometimes with permission and other times, through his alter ego as a white hat hacker. Now they knew who had stolen the fragments, Martin could trace Frik's path and discover who he worked for.

Jake was more determined than ever to find the pieces of the map and reach the Garden of Eden first.

CHAPTER 7

MARTIN KLEIN SAT IN the footwell of his desk, the wooden panels around and above him forming a kind of cocoon. He folded his tall frame into the tiny space, his knees up by his chin as he etched into the mahogany with a Swiss pocketknife, the blade kept sharp over the years for just such occasions.

Martin could have had one of the largest offices within the ARKANE Headquarters underneath Trafalgar Square in the heart of London. He certainly deserved it in his role as Head Librarian. He was unofficially known as the Brain of the Institute, responsible for the digital powerhouse of knowledge that ARKANE relied on for research. But while Martin easily lost himself in the technological world accessible through his fingertips and manageable with code, he sometimes found himself overwhelmed by the physical realm. This tiny space below his desk enabled him to enclose the vast universe in temporary walls while he focused on etching the lines that made life controllable — at least for a short time. The geometric constants of the square, the circle, the triangle. Over and over again.

A low beep came from his phone on the desk above.

Martin tilted his head to one side as the sound drew him from his concentrated reverie. It was the tone he had programmed for Morgan and Jake, the two ARKANE agents he considered closest to what some might call friends. They appreciated his way of being in the world, and he had followed them into danger many times with a trust born of experience and faith in their ability.

But something had changed in the last few months, and he wondered whether even they could manage what was to come.

Martin's job as archivist and librarian was far more than just managing the vast information storehouse. It was also seeking patterns in the material. His algorithms trawled the dark net as well as the various social media platforms, his bots burrowed into databases that governments thought to be unbreakable. His natural language processing engine, powered by the latest artificial intelligence, gathered words and phrases from diverse scanned images — ancient Sanskrit manuscripts in India, medieval biblical prophecy from plague times, banned books of the occult. In recent weeks, many of them pointed to something wild emerging, something savage on the horizon, something that could not be tamed by human endeavor.

That was why he had been driven under his desk once more. Martin rarely came across things he could not eventually understand, but this seemed beyond even his comprehension. He wanted to take his research to Director Marietti, but he didn't have a complete handle on it yet. It was as if there was some collective intelligence beneath it all, communicating across vast distances, slipping through his net of understanding.

The low beep came again.

Martin crawled out from under the desk and stood up, running his fingers through his shock of rough-cut blonde hair. It was particularly unruly today, spiking in all directions as a physical manifestation of his mental turmoil.

He picked up his phone and checked the message from Morgan. Tracing this Frik Versfeld would distract him for a little time at least. He sat down at his desk and dived into a world he could control.

* * *

Times Square, New York

Aurelia turned the corner of Broadway into the famous plaza at the heart of the city. The din of the crowd assaulted her senses, amplified by the honking of horns, the shouts of street vendors, the stink of fast food and the bright lights of the oversized digital screens beaming consumerism to the masses. Eager tourists flocked here from around the world, but Times Square was Aurelia's idea of hell. Her heart beat faster, her pulse raced, and she had to clench her fists to stop herself from running away from this cesspool.

She stood on the edge of the seething mass of humanity and closed her eyes, conjuring up the peace of the rainforest, the sound of birdsong, the scent of flowers after rain. The vision helped her to breathe more easily and strengthened her resolve. Today was important for the cause — the public face of it, anyway.

Aurelia glanced at her watch. It was almost time.

She pulled up the hood of her sweatshirt to hide her face and hurried toward the stand of seating where tourists watched a trio of lithe acrobats spin around and run up and down multi-colored poles. Their ability to move like monkeys across the branches of trees was such a contrast to the oversized tourists munching on fast food, oblivious to the damage they did to the world with every bite, unable to walk even a few blocks without a snack. They would not last long in a world without these comforts, and Aurelia couldn't help but smile at the thought of their suffering. After the way they treated Nature, it was time for payback.

She climbed to the highest part of the stand where she had a view over the entire square, trying to avoid touching the disgusting sea of bloated humanity along the way.

The giant digital screens above the throng suddenly turned black, the adverts silenced.

Tourists looked around in confusion, and even the street vendors and performers glanced up at the curious sight. Nothing usually prevented the constant flow of advertising in this area.

The screens flashed into life again — images of wild fires, gigantic mega storms, ice sheets tumbling into the ocean, bloated animal corpses, and sprawling cities pumping out toxic smoke and fumes into the atmosphere.

Destruction, annihilation, extinction. Humanity ravaging the Earth.

Aurelia watched with approval. Her wealth paid for the production and screen time, and while she appreciated the expertise of the organization, it was good to see they were spending it well. The video would now be dropped online and within minutes, it would spread around the world. While she instinctively hated the obtrusive control mechanisms of social media, Aurelia understood its power for spreading emotional messages to those who would never dream of doing their own research.

All around the square, people started dropping to the ground.

They lay on the pavement, bodies limp and unresponsive. One woman screamed as all those around her fell to the ground. She looked around in desperation, clearly thinking there was some kind of attack. Others dialed for the police as people around them continued to fall to the concrete.

The screens high above changed to display the logo of Gaia Insurgent over the images of continued destruction. A deep voice rang out across the square.

"Earth faces an existential crisis. If we do not stop this together, extinction threatens the entire planet. Today we perform a die-in across the world, members of Gaia Insurgent lie prone in public as a demonstration of extinction. Join us. Together we can save the world."

His voice faded out and the clamor of the crowd grew louder, even as bodies remained lying on the streets. Some bystanders nodded up in agreement at the images, some sat down cross-legged to join the protest. Others walked around the fake corpses, trying to pretend they did not even exist.

"They're just faking it," one man shouted as he threw a half-empty can of soda at one protestor. "Get up, you idiot."

He drew his leg back for a kick.

A hot dog vendor barged him sideways, so the blow didn't connect. "Leave him be. They're right. We are destroying the Earth. They're allowed to protest."

The man turned in anger and the resulting scuffle ignited those around them in confrontation. People shouted at each other, some coming to blows over their different views, while the protestors remained limp and motionless on the pavement below.

Aurelia watched with pleasure at the growing antagonism. People really would kill each other if the thin veneer of civilization was stripped away. *We are all just animals. We deserve the end that is coming for us.*

A siren rang out across the square, and police quickly advanced to dispel the troublemakers. They hauled the protestors to their feet, dragging them into vans as they pretended to be dead weight. Some would get booked, others would be released later on, many of them curiously proud to be facing penalties for civil disobedience.

These well-meaning members of Gaia Insurgent were happy to spend their weekends protesting and give money to plant more trees or save the burning animals, but most returned to comfy homes and middle-class lifestyles after their run-in with the law. They had the freedom to protest, the money to buy organic and ethical products while they criticized those who had no choice in how they lived. They were useful for the public face of the movement, but Aurelia was one of the few who understood the true goal. The

Revolutionaries of Gaia were willing to take things much further, for what could the planet become without people slashing and burning and polluting?

Aurelia was more than ready to die for her beliefs, and she was certain that the Earth would be better off without one particular species. It was only humanity that stood in the way of a thriving planet. Her hunt for Eden was just one of the ways that the Revolutionaries intended to pursue the end times. There was something special in the Garden, something that had the capacity to strike back, and Aurelia was determined to be the one to set it free.

Her phone buzzed with a text from Frik.

She smiled at the news of another recovered fragment. It wouldn't be long until they had them all and could trace a path to the Tree of Life. Aurelia looked out across the abomination of Times Square and imagined it full of bodies. The roots of trees grew over the corpses, and flowers bloomed from their remains as Nature ruled this land once more.

CHAPTER 8

IT DIDN'T TAKE LONG for Martin to find Frik Versfeld in the web of information at his fingertips. Once the South African had emerged from the field hospital at the mine, he took his payout and trained for the elite security services. There were images of Frik in the mountains of Pakistan alongside members of the Black Storks, in Russia with the Alpha Group and on civilian training exercises run by ex-US Navy SEALs. After working in several war zones, he re-entered the mining world in Brazil, running the security operation at Mina de Fidalgo.

There were suppressed police reports in the archives, complaints of brutal treatment of indigenous workers, and several women had turned up dead after being summoned to his lodgings. Martin clicked away from the disturbing images, pushing aside his concern for Morgan and Jake. They had dealt with such men before.

But one image in particular made his heart beat faster.

A painfully thin woman stood on the edge of a lush green rainforest, her chin raised in imperious determination. One of her hands lay flat on the bark of a tree, fingers spread out as if she were part of the forest. Aurelia dos Santos Fidalgo, the daughter of the mining magnate, who had recently inherited his empire. The article spoke of her determination to end the destruction of the rainforest by the mining industry and restore the damaged Earth. Frik worked as the head of her personal security, so she must be the true force behind the search for the map to Eden.

Martin frowned as he stared at Aurelia's face. He struggled to read people in the real world, often confused when the words they spoke did not match their actions or physical gestures. But this woman's singular purpose was clear. Her words matched her deeds, and her tenacity in her quest would not be stopped. The rainforest behind her looked wild and sinister, not the imagined haven that many considered it to be. ARKANE had faced religious fanatics before, but Aurelia was something different and Martin didn't quite know what to do with that.

He turned to his happy place, using the keyboard to enter a world of code. He was the master of this domain, and the hours passed quickly as he delved into an ever-widening web of possibilities for the location of the remaining fragments.

Martin started with the links between Macau and Amsterdam, expanding the map of the Portuguese Jewish Diaspora into places where the pieces might have ended up, ranking them according to the genealogy of the most likely families to have carried them.

When he had done as much as he could, he sent everything over to Morgan and Jake for review, along with the information on Frik and Aurelia. They would have to decide the next step in the hunt for the fragments — but Martin felt a pull of curiosity, a sense he had learned to trust over his many years working at ARKANE. Some vital piece of knowledge remained hidden just beyond his reach, and the one thing that Martin hated more than anything was a subject he could not master through his extensive archives.

ARKANE agents hunted down ancient manuscripts, medieval texts, secret libraries and religious relics so that all could be added to the vast storehouse of information held inside a complexity of databases, a tangle of ideas and threads of knowledge. But until every image and scrap of text was digitized, and every artifact scanned and catalogued, it would not be complete. It was Martin's life purpose to fill the gaps, and he used his hacking ability to stealthily access private collections and secret archives. Director Marietti helped by sending ARKANE agents after physical items, most of which were stored in the highly protected vault deep below his office. There should be an answer in here somewhere.

Martin followed his curiosity and dived into the most ancient manuscripts of the book of Genesis, searching for meaning behind the Tree of Life and translations of the text that might give an insight beyond the standard editions.

He started with the largest organized collection of Hebrew Old Testament manuscripts in the world, housed in the Russian National Library of St Petersburg. Martin accessed the Leningrad Codex, the oldest complete manuscript of the Hebrew Bible dated around 1008 CE and brought up scanned images of the text. His fingers flashed across the keyboard as he delved into the Aleppo Codex, held at the Shrine of the Book in Jerusalem, and then put both images on the screen side by side. He added the oldest Greek version from the fifth-century Codex Alexandrinus and finally, the earliest Aramaic version, the London Palimpsest 5b1.

Martin scanned the translations, speed reading the commentary from different scholars. The frown deepened in his brow as he realized how many different views there were on something as fundamental as how God might have created the world.

The five books of the Pentateuch — Genesis, Exodus, Leviticus, Numbers and Deuteronomy — had been created from two primary sources with repeated stories, like the two creation passages, used to separate them.

While it was originally thought that the Yahwist wrote from the time of the kings, perhaps even from the court of Solomon, more recent scholarship placed it during the Babylonian exile of the sixth century BCE. The Priestly aspects of the Pentateuch were generally considered to be created later in the period of exile, or afterward as the ancient Jews codified their religion.

After several more hours of the minutiae of textual analysis, Martin admitted defeat. His true gift was finding connections across diverse sources, not delving deep into a few chapters of one particular faith. He could lose himself in biblical scholarship and religious arguments that raged over centuries — or he could find himself an expert. While Morgan and Jake traced the path of the map, he would focus on finding the location of Eden from a scholarly angle. There was one person he knew that might be able to help him take the next step.

*   *   *

MGM Cotai, Macau

Morgan stepped out of what was possibly the most luxurious bathroom she had ever experienced in what was most definitely the fluffiest hotel robe she had ever worn. Her dark hair hung in wet curls around her face, all traces of ash and smoke washed from her body. The medics had checked her over, but she only had bruises from the fall and some minor burns, nothing compared to her injuries from past missions.

Jake had taken the brunt of the damage this time around. He was resting up in the adjoining room after being released from hospital while they both enjoyed the hospitality of one of the best hotels in Macau. ARKANE didn't always stretch the budget to this level of extravagance, but Morgan was grateful for the chance to retreat away from the busy city streets.

She walked over to the wall of glass that dominated the Sky Loft room and looked out across the skyscrapers of Macau, each one representing thousands of people come to gamble and shop and experience the excesses of wealth for even a short time. Morgan could just glimpse the Zhujiang River Estuary in the distance, but other than that tiny strip of blue, there was very little of nature here. Much of the land had been reclaimed from the waters with large amounts of rock or cement dumped into the coastline, infilling with clay and soil until the desired height had been reached. More space for rising consumerism, more opportunities to spend, more experiences to enjoy. And who was she to question such desire? Morgan gave a wry smile as she sank down onto the incredibly comfortable king-sized bed.

Her phone pinged with a message. The latest research from Martin Klein.

There was a dossier on Frik Versfeld and pictures of him as a good-looking young man working the mines of South Africa. One image showed him laughing as he worked, and it was hard to reconcile his smiling face with the nightmare of scarred rage who emerged from the flames in the burning church. The man who had tortured and murdered Ines.

Morgan read of Jake's part in the mining accident and how the injuries shaped Frik's path into increasingly shady security companies, laid off for violence and abuse until eventually, he was hired for that very brutality.

She sighed as she thought of Jake lying in the next room. They had both been on missions that resulted in death and destruction, they both had to weigh up the greater good — and they both made mistakes. Yet Morgan hoped, on balance, that they managed to stay on the side of the angels. Each must choose their path, and every day brought the opportunity to move toward good or evil. Jake had made a mistake back then, but Frik had chosen his own direction.

She laid the information aside and read about the woman Frik worked for. Aurelia dos Santos Fidalgo, heiress of a mining empire, was dangerously thin, her face pinched, and yet she exuded confidence in official photos with tailored suits and striking makeup that made her look every inch the entitled, wealthy businesswoman.

But there were other photos that Martin had sourced from social media and intelligence reports. Aurelia in baggy jeans and a hooded sweatshirt, bare-faced and wearing a baseball cap and dark glasses at Gaia Insurgent marches in Brazil and other international locations. One picture even showed her in a crowd blockading the mining trucks of her own company. She stood on the edge of the group, out of range of the mainstream media outlets, careful to avoid notice. But no one can escape the phone camera in every pocket these days.

Martin had also included evidence of financial transfers from Aurelia's private accounts to eco-terrorist organizations. Morgan wondered what the Board of the Fidalgo mining company would think of Aurelia's true allegiance. It would surely be enough to remove her from the company, and that was powerful information to have.

She put the pictures aside and read about the incredible journeys of the Portuguese Diaspora and the other possible locations for the pieces of the Eden manuscript.

One particular report caught her eye from a most unusual place. Truth it seemed was even stranger than fiction. She would have Martin lay a false trail to keep Frik off their scent for now. It would slow him down and give them time to find the next fragment.

As Morgan read on, she knew that it wouldn't be long until they left the luxury of this hotel. She reached over and dialed room service. Might as well enjoy it while it lasted.

*   *   *

John Soane Museum, London

Martin walked into the grand square of Lincoln's Inn Fields, a little wet after his brisk walk from Trafalgar Square at the tail end of a rainstorm. He shook out his umbrella, grateful for both its protection from the weather but also for keeping his fellow Londoners from walking too close. The busy city was his home, but he preferred the quiet solitude of his office and control over his personal space.

He stopped in front of a terraced house with high, arched windows, its white facade enhanced by partial columns in the Grecian style. Statues on the third level balcony looked out over the square with contempt for modernity, as if they could see back to when the painter JMW Turner came to call on the architect Sir John Soane.

But Martin was not here for the past.

Sir Sebastian Northbrook was the curator of the John Soane Museum and also its heir, although the fortune had been gifted to the nation in 1833, so he couldn't touch the vast resources except to maintain the grand house and its collection.

Martin had met Sebastian on the night Morgan searched the Grand Lodge of England for a piece of the Ark of the Covenant. He shuddered as he remembered the dense smoke and how the flames had lit up the night sky. Sebastian had risked his life to save Morgan and almost died in the conflagration, but somehow Martin had found the strength to pull him out.

A few weeks later, Sebastian had emerged from intensive care and Martin visited him in the day ward. He felt responsible somehow, like a piece of his soul entwined itself with Sebastian's that night. Since then, he had found himself walking over to the museum at odd hours to check on the hardy old man — and to pick his brain. While Martin had mastered the art of querying databases and linking together ideas across space and time, he still marveled at how one human brain could encompass so much seemingly useless knowledge and still pull out astounding facts or an opinion on possibilities that his own machine creations could not fathom. Sebastian's unique perspective often helped with a conundrum, and he was also very well connected. Martin was in need of a new perspective on the puzzle of Eden, and he hoped his friend could help.

It was out of hours and the museum was closed, so Martin rang the bell with a series of jabs, a code they had agreed on. Sebastian did not like cold callers, and Martin certainly agreed with that.

A minute later, the door opened and Sebastian beckoned him in. His thin, angular frame seemed more gaunt than usual in his tailored Savile Row suit, his white hair combed into a neat side parting that he had likely worn since his early days at Eton and Oxford. But Martin saw beyond the exterior of the British aristocrat. Sebastian had a wicked sense of humor and a fondness for cognac that he only revealed to those he considered friends.

"Come in, dear fellow." Sebastian walked ahead of Martin down the hall. "I just put together a cheese platter with more than enough for two. We shall dine in the company of the gods."

The museum was a strange labyrinth of unusual treasures collected over John Soane's career. The son of a bricklayer who rose to become a professor of architecture at the Royal Academy and an official architect to the Office of Works, Soane was knighted for his services in 1831. He had redesigned the interior of this building to house his collection and in the daylight, sun streamed in through light wells, reflected in a series of mirrors into even the most hidden nooks and crannies.

Sebastian led the way to the gallery where a small round table sat underneath the watchful gaze of the lion-headed goddess Sekhmet. Casts of classical figures lined the walls, each a representation of an ancient god. They overlooked the pride of the museum, an Egyptian sarcophagus of Seti I from 1370 BCE, purchased by Soane when the British Museum declined it for lack of funds. The translucent alabaster shone under artful lighting, revealing traces of a carving within. The goddess Nut who ruled the sky and the night, protecting the dead as they entered the afterlife.

Sebastian sat down at the table and pulled a perfectly folded napkin onto his lap, indicating that Martin do the same.

The cheese platter was a thing of beauty. Three perfect wedges sat upon a Chinese circular porcelain dish inlaid with midnight blue engraving. Cornish Yarg wrapped in wild garlic leaves, Tunworth Camembert, and Stichelton blue lay next to an artfully arranged selection of crackers and a sliver of quince paste. Two glasses of port sat in the correct glasses next to dainty plates.

There was no rushing Sebastian when it came to cheese, so Martin waited until they had eaten a little and toasted the health of the monarch before explaining why he had come.

"The Garden of Eden," Sebastian said, with wonder in his voice. "You truly think it might exist?"

Martin shrugged. "Honestly, I don't know. But there are archaeological records of ancient gardens in the Middle East. Perhaps it is not so far-fetched to imagine some ancestral Eden."

Sebastian stood up and walked to the edge of the gallery, his slim fingers clutching the edge of the parapet. By his rigid pose and white knuckles, Martin could see his friend was conflicted, so he waited in silence. That was the best way he knew for allowing people time to process. Sometimes he could sit in silence on his own for many hours, and he was patient enough to do it for a friend.

When Sebastian finally turned, his jaw was set with

determination. "There is someone who might be able to help. I haven't seen her for many years but perhaps it's time I returned to Paris…"

As his words trailed off, Martin saw a trace of concern pass over his friend's face. Whoever they would meet on the next step of the journey clearly had some hold over him, and Martin could only wonder what that might be.

CHAPTER 9

Adana, Turkey

As the sun reached its zenith, Guram entered the agricultural complex. He had recovered from his injuries and his mornings were once again spent in prayer and study. There was much to learn in his path through the ranks of the Brotherhood, but the Order was not just about books and learning, it was also about practical work and commerce. Today's meeting could be lucrative indeed.

He pulled thick gloves from his pocket, the leather well-worn and molded to his hands. He would never dare to enter without these and other protection against Her many ways of stinging, pricking or poisoning.

People out there in the world thought nothing of sampling berries from hedgerows or foraging for mushrooms, boiling up strange leaves for tea without knowing that one mistake could kill them and their children. A crimson seed might stop the heart, an innocent-looking leaf brushing the skin might cause an eruption of blisters, tea brewed from bark might blind a man.

Those who considered Mother Nature to be gentle and loving, cradling humankind in Her bosom, did not understand all the ways She could kill. But Guram understood that the snake at the heart of the Garden was Nature Herself, betrayer of all that God wanted for man. She was here first, before Adam took his first step, and all who followed merely tried to loosen Her deadly grip.

Guram walked to the corner of the garden where a corpse flower bloomed. He stood in front of it and breathed in the foul odor of a rotting body, letting his body steep in revulsion, revisiting his fear from the dark moments in Eden. This was the true side of Nature, and his hate hardened as the stench sank into his skin.

The scent of flowers was to some a delight, but Guram understood that it was only a lure to attract insects to serve their purpose. The smell was a fetid miasma, a stink of fecundity. Some out there in the world found gardens to be pleasant places of peace and harmony, but they did not see the maggots devouring decayed flesh beneath the soil, the roots of trees reaching blindly out to tap into precious water, and beetles scuttling amongst leaf rot. Nature was crawling, creeping, wriggling, strangling death — and the Brotherhood existed to keep Her contained.

When the Catholic Church had disavowed the Order and cut off their funding hundreds of years ago, the Brothers used their knowledge of the deadly side of plants to provide poisons, chemical weapons, toxins, and even assassination for hire. There were many who wanted to wield the deadly side of Nature against their foes and have the evidence disappear back into the earth.

Over many generations, the Order purchased land and expanded their holdings, navigating the tangled web of international commerce, weaving ancient and modern into a thriving Brotherhood. These days, under a tangle of shell companies and not-for-profit corporations, the Order of the Ignis Flammae was wealthier than a small nation state.

This agricultural complex on the outskirts of Adana, Turkey, was one of the most profitable. It benefitted from the large fertile plain of Çukurova that supported one of the oldest continually inhabited settlements in the world, once a regional center for the powerful Ottoman Empire. Millions of people lived in the region, so they had plenty of eager workers who would not ask too many questions.

The Order had such agricultural land all over the world, where the Brothers raised crops that would serve their purpose before cutting them down, grinding them into pulp and using them to serve mankind as Mother Nature should always have done. The one plant they did not cultivate was the tree that grew in the Garden of Eden, a place protected by the Ignis Flammae for generations. The Brotherhood's holy mission was to ensure that none would ever find it, for to liberate Nature from Her bonds would be to damn humanity forever.

Guram looked out at the vast expanse of the estate, separated into different areas that controlled the eco-systems and prevented cross-contamination. By means of specialist glasshouses and terrariums, they replicated different environments and grew a countless species of trees and plants.

One field was dedicated to cultivating ergot, *Claviceps purpurea*, a toxic fungus that grew on wheat and rye. It could cause seizures, nausea, gangrene and death, but could also lead to hallucinations, hysteria, and a sensation of skin crawling, all of which led to it being a possible trigger for the Salem witch trials sparked by young girls behaving in a way that could not be explained.

The Ignis Flammae had used ergot through the ages to control villages throughout Europe, punishing them for sin by cultivating the crop locally. A mania would seize the people, sometimes known as St Anthony's fire, as they danced to try and escape the burning of their flesh.

One particular area of the complex focused on cultivating fungi. They had plenty of death caps, responsible for around ninety percent of all mushroom deaths around the world. Even a small dose could permanently damage the kidneys and liver, and the Brothers had regular clients for the crop. There was a special place for the hallucinogenic magic mushroom with varying levels of psilocybin. This particular trade had grown over recent years with the popularity of micro-dosing amongst the tech community after famous names indulged at the Burning Man festival in the Nevada desert. Guram smiled at the zigzag of history, how mankind had embraced and rejected natural drugs so many times over millennia, and throughout, the Order had been there to service the need as it arose.

Officials had inspected the farms over the years, and most had been satisfied with a cursory look at the public-facing side of the monastery, but some had questioned the need to grow such toxic and dangerous plants. They fulfilled their destiny as fertilizer sooner than they might have expected. After all, the garden could be a dangerous place.

Guram walked through a warehouse past one of the processing areas. Most workers were local men from villages surrounding the area. They had no idea where these packages would go, no inkling of the destruction that followed in the wake of the powders and infusions and bark shavings they sent out each day.

There were other parts of the garden where the Order cultivated plants for pleasure. Smoky tobacco, peppery betel nuts, the bitter coca leaf, all purveyors of bliss and pain, profit and power throughout the world. The Brothers refined varieties to enhance their addictive properties, driving revenue into holding companies that owned vast shares in those organizations that peddled the resulting products to the masses.

Then there were plants that enabled man to transcend the physical body. The woody bark of the ayahuasca vine, *Banisteriopsis caapi*, mixed with the potent leaves of chacruna, *Psychotria viridis*, could alter the mind so the seeker could experience God. But it was not the God that Guram knew, merely the trickster Herself playing with their minds.

These plants could make a person feel that they were one with the world, and some emerged from such trances with a deep love for Nature, and a passion for preserving Her. She wound Her way into their hearts, disguising Her true purpose, which is why the Brothers were not allowed to partake. It was forbidden to draw closer to the Temptress without adequate protection in place.

Guram was grateful that She couldn't hide Herself entirely, that bad trips consumed some with tangles of dark creatures, hooked claws and razor fangs tearing at their consciousness. But still, they sought Her.

He hated those particular plants and wished he could destroy them all, but he was a practical man. They were part of the Order's income, funding their expansion, and he was ever committed to the cause.

Today he had a returning client, a discerning buyer from England known only as Attercop. Guram knew that the man was some kind of broker for the aristocracy and he had once tried to find out more. But when he discovered that the man's name came from the Old Norse and High German words for poisonous ulcer, and the Middle English for poison-head spider, he stopped looking. The less he knew about his clients, the better.

Attercop stood near a small hardwood tree, bending his compact frame to examine the under-ripe green fruit, thin lips pursed in displeasure. He turned on Guram's approach and the man's unusual appearance struck the monk once more. His head was almost triangular, with a huge forehead made even more prominent by a receding hairline. His features all lay in the bottom half of his face, bisected by thick black glasses that couldn't quite hide the pale cysts that grew around his eyes. As usual, he wore an impeccably tailored three-piece suit in elegant charcoal, utterly out of place in this area of the world. But Guram didn't think anyone would question Attercop's taste for long.

"Don't get too close," he said. "That's a suicide tree, *Cerbera odollam*. The fruit looks like a mango when ripe and the toxins from the seeds don't show up in normal toxicology reports."

Attercop raised an eyebrow and then shook his head. "Too exotic."

"You have a particular... project in mind?"

Attercop nodded. "The subject in question enjoys being out in nature. She's elderly but extremely well protected. She controls a vast estate and her son has had enough of waiting. It must be a naturally explainable death."

Guram smiled. "Let me show you some options."

He walked on through the garden to an area of raised beds, cultivated with some of their most popular specimens.

Guram pointed at one plant with spiked blue flowers shaped like a hood. "*Aconitum napellus*, wolfsbane or monkshood. Its toxin asphyxiates by paralyzing the nerves and stopping the heart. Aconitine is so powerful that it formed the spit of the hell-hound Cerberus from Greek mythology and the Nazis used it in poisoned bullets."

Attercop took a small red notebook from his inside jacket pocket, along with a fountain pen of slightly tarnished silver. He made a few notes, then nodded. "What else?"

Guram continued. "Do you know of the British journalist murdered by a puncture wound from an umbrella while walking across Waterloo Bridge in London back in the 70s?"

Attercop nodded. "I believe he was a Communist defector murdered by the Russians. Ricin, wasn't it?"

Guram nodded. "Yes, the man died of multiple haemorrhages with almost every organ affected." He pointed at a nearby shrub. Splashes of burgundy highlighted its leaves and prickly seedpods rose in bulbous globes. "This is the castor bean plant, *Ricinus communis*. It's a laxative in small doses with the ricin removed and reduces inflammation when used externally. But a batch that still contains the ricin might be effective for your purpose."

Attercop leaned in to look more closely, careful not to touch the plant. "I couldn't get near enough to the target for such a puncture to occur."

Guram walked around the raised bed to a low-growing, carpet-like plant with tiny yellow flowers. He pulled back the segmented leaves to reveal a small swelling fruit with wicked spines at its tip. "This is puncture vine, *Tribulus terrestris*. It's strong enough to pierce rubber and even leather and easily penetrates bare skin."

Attercop smiled in a way that made Guram repress a shiver as he continued.

"It can be used as a natural delivery system. Just coat the spikes and leave on a regularly used path, or perhaps in an area where someone might come in from the outside and take off their shoes—"

"Thinking they're safe," Attercop finished for him. "But the danger is inside all along." He nodded. "That is a definite possibility. I'll take several batches of both." He wrote something in his notebook and then looked up with expectation.

Guram led him over to a freestanding timber frame wound through with a woody vine with thick stems and wide glossy leaves. "*Chondrodendron tomentosum*, commonly known as curare. Often used for hunting by native tribes, its muscle relaxant properties paralyze prey when it enters the bloodstream."

Attercop snorted a little. "I'm hardly going to shoot the old woman with a poisoned dart, am I?"

Guram gave a half-smile. "In the late 1800s and early nineteenth century, doctors used it to keep a patient still during surgery. With artificial respiration to keep them alive, they would feel every cut, every slice, while unable to move or scream. I thought it might be useful to you."

Attercop looked intently at the vine, his eyes seeing beyond it to some dark future. "Hmm, you're right. That could be interesting for a different project. I'll take some of that, too."

In his head, Guram calculated the potential value of the transaction. Although their ultimate treasure was in Heaven, it was still important to show dedication by bringing in money to the Order. He would be doubly blessed if he could show the Abbot evidence of his singular devotion.

Guram led the man over to a shrub around five feet high with round black berries. "This is coyotillo, *Karwinskia humboldtiana*. It causes paralysis and death, but not straight away. The weakness starts in the feet and legs and slowly brings the respiratory system to a halt."

"I'll definitely take some of that."

As Attercop wrote more notes, Guram noticed the Abbot beckoning from a shaded area in the far corner of the garden. His heart beat faster as he considered the possibility of what he might be called for. Peddling the poisons of Nature was satisfying but ultimately beneath him, and he longed for a mission worthy of his true potential.

He quickly showed Attercop the last samples and then left the man in the capable hands of one of the other Brothers who would finalize the details of invoicing and delivery.

Once the English assassin was out of sight, Guram hurried over to the arbor where the Abbot sat on a carved wooden bench.

"It is time, my son." The old man's expression was grim, and the shadows under his eyes had deepened with the burden he clearly carried. The Abbot touched the cord around his neck, his fingers running down to cup the silver pendant at its base. "You must go out into the world and walk amongst the fallen. The fragments are in danger of being gathered together, and there is a woman, a professor, who might be able to discern the meaning of it. She must not be allowed to see the map."

Guram found it hard to control his disgust as the Abbot spoke of such a creature. The woman Eve had been responsible for sin in the Garden, and even though all men were born from women, he wished it did not have to be so. The Garden caused the sin of Eve, and it had turned a sacred place of God into wild Nature that the Brothers now battled daily to keep in check.

He pointed to the beds of virulent poisonous plants. "Shall I use something that cannot be traced?"

The Abbot shook his head. "Don't kill her. Not yet. I must understand what she knows first, and then we will offer her to the Garden. It is only fitting for one with such knowledge. Bring her to me at Eden."

Guram nodded. "Where is she?"

The Abbot shook his head, melancholy shrouding his expression. "I'm sorry, my son, but you must go to a city of great sin. You must go to Paris."

CHAPTER 10

FRIK VERSFELD STORMED OUT of the terminal building at Goa International Airport, India, his fists clenched in annoyance at the barely tolerable flight. There were many things he hated about long-distance travel, but at least he might be able to work out his frustration on Jake Timber's face soon enough.

Aurelia's team of hackers had found evidence of multiple bookings for the pair of ARKANE agents out of Macau, an obvious attempt to throw him off their trail. But one route had been booked under fake names and Frik had decided that Goa was their most likely destination since it also fit with the history of the Portuguese in this area of the world.

The other options were Jamaica in the Caribbean, which seemed ridiculous as it wasn't even a former Portuguese territory — and Luanda in Angola, which Frik remembered with some fondness.

His bank account had been nicely padded while working there during the last years of the civil war, which stretched on for 27 years after the country's independence from Portugal. The lack of oversight from his oil company employers allowed Frik the freedom to experiment with new methods of torture, and the women were desperate enough for his dollars that they endured his particular brand of pleasure.

Luanda was one of the most expensive cities in the world, but there was a stark division between the rich in their luxury gated compounds and the poor in the stinking slums. The place was still chaotic in the wake of the conflict and Frik could see no reason why a relic of the Jews would be kept somewhere so desperate. Goa had to be the place. He jumped in a taxi and headed for Goa Velha, the old city and former capital of Portuguese India.

Frik emerged in front of the extravagant Baroque-style facade of the Basilica of Bom Jesus with its four towering levels in red brick and white marble. Two smaller entrances flanked an enormous door, thronged by the faithful who gathered to see the patron saint of Goa, St Francis Xavier. His mortal remains rested within, apparently still incorrupt after five hundred years, and his tomb seemed like a reasonable place to keep a relic — or the fragment of an ancient map.

Frik steeled himself against the mass of humanity around him as he strode toward the entrance. Indians had no sense of personal space, and it was all he could do to restrain himself from shouting at the bastards to get out of his way. He kept an eye out for the figures of Jake and Morgan, but they were nowhere to be seen. He must have beaten them here.

The spacious interior of the basilica had high ceilings, wide windows and cream walls with an extravagant altar of gold with paintings of angels singing Gloria to God. Frik had to hand it to the Catholics. They really did have some impressive architecture.

Tourists crowded around a side altar where a gigantic Florentine mausoleum stood, covered with ornate carvings of stars and cherubs. The body of St Francis lay inside a casket within. The faithful here honored the saint, but many others considered him responsible for the torture and death of thousands as he had requested the Inquisition come to India in 1545. The records had been conveniently lost over time, but many died here, burned alive in the fires of the auto-da-fé.

Frik had no personal faith in God, but he did have an appreciation for the various branches of the Inquisition.

They had perfected the art of torture and the merciless killing of those they considered less than true believers, and they were certainly right to consider women inferior beings. Frik sometimes grated at working for Aurelia, but she had starved herself into looking nothing like a real woman, and she was as ruthless as a man on behalf of her cause. She might even have made a good Inquisitor. Frik smiled at the image of the gaunt heiress with a red-hot poker in her hand, advancing on those she wished to wipe off the face of the Earth — and there were many of those, that was certain.

He also had great respect for the Portuguese explorers who headed out to conquer foreign lands, who had reshaped the world in their own image, transforming the territories they possessed and whose heritage still resounded in the modern world. Frik rejected those bed-wetting commentators who thought that reparations should be paid for past atrocities. Couldn't they see how much the Europeans had done for these cesspools of humanity?

He finally made it to the front of the pack of believers and stared at the ridiculously ornate casket containing the remains of the saint. Frik realized that there was no way he was getting into that thing without a serious amount of explosive. As much as he enjoyed blowing things up, there was something not quite right about the situation.

As he walked away from the basilica, Frik wondered where the hell the ARKANE agents could be. There were few other places that made sense here in Goa. Perhaps he had made the wrong choice after all?

No matter. Aurelia would find out where they were soon enough, and he would go beat the hell out of the smug bastard who had scarred him. Jake Timber would leave the world looking a lot less pretty than he did now.

* * *

As the cargo plane banked over the azure waves of the Caribbean, Morgan considered how small the world felt when you could cross it in a day. The Portuguese explorers on their ships would not have been able to travel both east and west from their home ports as she did so easily. Most of them died far from their homelands in countries they claimed for their king, disregarding the people who already lived in the lands they conquered.

There were so many incredible things about the modern world, so much to discover and experience. Some thought there was little mystery left, that everything could be found through the portal of an internet search, online video and social media, but that was merely a curated and edited version of the real world. To understand a place or a people, you had to walk the streets. If you wanted to know the truth behind the facade, you had to dig much deeper than what could be found through a screen. Morgan was grateful for this because, let's face it, if Martin and his vast digital power could solve all ARKANE's problems, then she and Jake would be out of a job. Then what would she do with her life?

The shores of Jamaica came into view, the green mountainous regions of the inner island visible across white sand beaches and the modern city of Kingston. The plane flew in over Port Royal and bumped a little on landing. As the roar of the engines fell silent, Morgan sighed with relief. Cargo planes were the most efficient way of getting from Macau to Jamaica, but they were not designed for a pleasant flight. The luxurious memory of the MGM Cotai had faded with the first few hours of flying, and now she was desperate to get off.

Jake unfolded himself from a padded bench, yawning as he sat up and unstrapped the various loops he'd constructed to keep himself in place during the flight. He moved with some residual discomfort and gently touched his ribs.

"How are you feeling?" Morgan asked.

Jake took a deep breath and then coughed a little as the pain clearly intensified. "Not quite one hundred percent, but getting there. The long sleep helped. Did you get some rest?"

She shrugged. "A little, but I did a *lot* of reading."

Jake smiled. "Excellent, but we need coffee before we tackle the library."

Morgan smiled at the thought. Jamaica was famous for its Blue Mountain blends. "Definitely."

They emerged from the plane into a different kind of heat than Macau, with a stiff ocean breeze blowing clouds across the sky and refreshing the surrounding air. Airports were similar all over the world, but the faces here were different and the atmosphere was more relaxed. Macau had a frenzied underlying sense of commerce. If you didn't hustle, you wouldn't make it to the end of the day. Kingston seemed more about just letting the day happen around you, and as they walked through the terminal, Morgan relaxed a little. This wasn't such a bad place to investigate where the next piece of the map might be.

They jumped in a taxi and headed around the bay into the city, stopping at a coffee shop near the Kingston library. Morgan sat at a table outside in the early morning sun while Jake ordered the local brew. A little further down the street, a man cooked on half a metal drum while local workers gathered around, enticed by the sweet smell of fried plantain and johnny cakes, little fried dumplings served alongside akee fruit and salt-fish.

Jake emerged from the shop with an easy smile on his face and steaming cups of coffee in his hands. "This is more like home for me, more like Africa. I love it already."

Morgan took a sip of the black coffee and allowed her body to loosen up in the sun. The city was not quite as she had expected. There were modern office buildings next to tin shacks, tiny stores selling different goods with makeshift tarpaulins as shade, a juxtaposition of wealth and poverty.

The culture was a world away from Macau, but the disparity between rich and poor was just as evident.

"There doesn't seem to be much here of the Portuguese?" Jake noted as he stretched out his legs.

"That's because the Spanish were here, not the Portuguese," Morgan said, recalling the information Martin had sent. "They arrived in 1494 when Christopher Columbus claimed this area, and most of the indigenous people died of diseases brought by the sailors. The Spanish brought many thousands of African slaves to the island to work the fields, and the population grew. The British conquered it in 1655 and expanded the sugar plantations. After slaves were emancipated in 1838, many of the freedmen continued to work on subsistence farms. Jamaica became independent from the United Kingdom in 1962 but is still part of the Commonwealth."

Jake looked confused. "So why are we here then?"

Morgan gave a broad smile. "Jewish pirates of the Caribbean."

CHAPTER 11

Paris, France

THE CRISP AIR HAD a bite from the easterly wind that swept the first fallen leaves from the ground and whirled them in the air as Martin and Sebastian hurried along the Rue de Richelieu toward the Bibliothèque Nationale, the national library of France. They had taken the earliest Eurostar, just two-and-a-half hours from London, arriving in time for coffee and *pain au chocolat* before heading out into the bustling city.

Sebastian's silver-topped cane clicked rhythmically on the flagstones as they passed the thriving local shops. He didn't need it for leaning on; the man was fit as a fiddle, but Martin suspected the cane held some hidden weapon or other unusual feature that made it indispensable on such a journey.

Although he usually preferred to stay away from so many people, Martin loved Paris. There was something about the language that made his mind turn in a different way, and he loved to sound out the words in his head as they passed shop signs: *numismatique, laverie, laboratoire d'analyses medicales*. The syllables were pleasing in their difference to English and, even though his French was passable, Martin found that he didn't tune in so much to the rest of the world when people spoke an unfamiliar language around him.

He could relax and walk and experience the morning. Bells ringing on bikes and scooters rushing by with a muted roar. The smell of freshly baked baguettes and sugar-topped pastries wafting from a boulangerie underneath apartments with filigree balconies. It was good to walk in a city that was so close to London and yet so distant in terms of culture. Martin regretted the choice of the British people to exit Europe in a practical sense, but he would never leave it in his heart.

Sebastian was quieter than his usual ebullient self, and his fingers clutched the top of his cane with white knuckles. He hadn't said much about who they were visiting, just that she was a preeminent biblical scholar, someone he had known many years ago and whose career he had followed from afar. As they approached the entrance to the Bibliothèque Nationale, his usually pale skin flushed a little in expectation. Martin grew increasingly curious, but he would not ask about it. The ways of people were endlessly varied, and he had learned over many years of puzzlement to wait and watch and observe.

The sound of laughter and lively chatter came from a leafy park opposite the entrance to the library. Groups of students sat on the grass around an ornate fountain, making the most of the autumn sun as they relaxed next to an immense oak tree that could have been planted back when the library was established at this site in the seventeenth century.

Martin had done his research on the place, preferring to know exactly what he was walking into. He had studied the history of the library and the physical layout of the Richelieu site, as well as hacking into its security to check for any issues. He found their system to be adequate for a place of learning, but while he was in there, he added various things that would help the French if someone other than a white hat hacker came their way.

The National Library of France traced its beginnings to

the books collected by King Charles V in 1368 and originally held at the Louvre Palace. Known as the *Bibliothèque du Roi*, the library of the King, the collection grew over generations as it moved to various locations. It opened to the public in 1692 and expanded under the French Revolution when private collections of aristocrats were seized, and it became known as the *Bibliothèque Nationale*, the property of the French people rather than the crown. Napoleon increased its holdings and by 1896, it was the world's largest repository of books. The ravages of the Second World War laid waste to its collection, but the library expanded after liberation, and in the 1980s it became one of the largest and most modern libraries in the world.

Despite its modernity and France's rejection of its regal beginnings, Martin couldn't help but be glad of the library's aristocratic heritage, for without the empire of the rich, it would not be housed in the gorgeous Richelieu building which had only recently reopened in full after several years of restoration.

The tricolor flag of the French Republic flew above the oversized doorway next to the blue standard of the European Union with its twelve gold stars representing unity, solidarity and harmony. Sebastian led the way into a large courtyard beyond, with Martin following close behind.

* * *

Guram stood under the oak tree, watching as the two men entered the library. One was old and thin, the other bespectacled, both built for desk work. Neither would be a problem.

He leaned back against the trunk and used the wood to press his clothes against his skin. Under his modern t-shirt and jeans, he wore a thin forest green vest woven through with thorns to remind him of his purpose. As the tiny hooks cut into his flesh, he relished the task ahead. He had never witnessed a woman given to the Garden before, but he heard from one Brother that it would be worth the wait. The screams from a daughter of Eve refreshed the soul in a way that no other sacrifice could. Nature devouring what She had created in a perfect circle. Guram sighed in anticipation as he texted Brother Hadiq who waited around the block with a van ready for transport.

A group of students laughed nearby, their faces transformed by the sun into the epitome of carefree humanity. They sat on manicured grass surrounded by ornate flower beds. They walked in constricted and controlled Nature, and they could not fathom the danger they faced if She was let loose upon the world. Guram hoped they would never know, and his job today was making sure that Eden could not be discovered in this generation.

He pushed away from the tree and slowly followed the two men into the library, retracing the steps he had already taken in the early hours of the morning to lay his trap.

* * *

Martin and Sebastian passed through the main entrance beneath a chandelier that hung low from the high ceiling and walked on through the corridors until they reached the Labrouste Reading Room. Martin stopped to gaze up at its vaulted roof, supported by slender iron pillars with decorative filigree flanked by six stories of book stacks. Nine domes painted in muted shades of terracotta and ivory arched above, each topped with glass so that light flooded the space, making the room a true architectural splendor.

Students sat at desks, heads bent over their books, and Martin thought that he could never concentrate in such a place. He would look up at the sky through the high windows and marvel at the way the light played over so many volumes of learning. He spent his days in the buried rooms of ARKANE under Trafalgar Square and for a moment, he dreamed that perhaps he could have a sky office, one with a view of the heavens.

"There she is." Sebastian's words were soft, almost a sigh. They captured a sense of unspoken history, as if he had been waiting for her all his life.

Martin followed his gaze across the library. A woman stood under one of the arches wearing a tailored grey suit and towering stiletto heels that only served to emphasize her trim figure in a way that French women mastered from a young age. Her profile was regal, like an African matriarch used to commanding armies, her makeup perfectly applied to highlight her petite features. Martin recalled her face from the research he had done on the library. Professor Camara Mbaye, a French-Senegalese biblical scholar who also specialized in paleo-botany, the evolutionary history of plants and the biological reconstruction of past environments.

Camara looked across the room and her gaze alighted on Sebastian. She stood a little taller, her dark eyes fixed on his face and as she smiled, a ray of sun illuminated the library with its warmth.

Sebastian walked toward her and she toward him. When they met in the center of the Reading Room, it was as if no one else existed. Their eyes locked onto one another, oblivious to the surrounding students. Camara walked into Sebastian's arms and hugged him, kissing him on both cheeks. He held her for a moment longer than strictly friends would and just before she pulled away, she whispered something. Martin couldn't hear the words, but when Sebastian turned to beckon him over, his cheeks were aflame with a blush.

Once they were all outside the quiet of the Reading Room, Sebastian introduced them both, emphasizing Martin's expertise in research and his position at ARKANE and Camara's extensive knowledge.

"What brings you to Paris, Sebastian?" she asked. "It's been a long time since we saw each other."

"Too long," Sebastian said. "I didn't know if you would forgive—"

Camara cut him off with a wave of her hand and a shake of her head. "The past is past. I do not live with regret." She looked at Martin. "Tell me what you need. I know a little of what you do at ARKANE and I have to admit, it intrigues me."

"We need help to locate the Garden of Eden." As Martin spoke the words aloud, he realized how crazy it sounded.

Camara laughed with delight. "Ah, this is a true quest and one that all have failed at so far." Her dark eyes twinkled. "But you've come to the right place. I uncovered some fascinating clues at a dig in northern Iran last summer. Then my funding ran out, our local fixer disappeared, and they revoked my permits. I had to leave quickly, but the run of bad luck makes me even more curious. Come, I'll show you."

Camara led them away from the grand historical section of the library to a more functional wing where doors opened off a long corridor. Martin itched to see inside these rooms, aware of the treasures held within that he longed to add to his vast collection. Not all the knowledge of the world had been scanned and so much was inaccessible to his powerful algorithms — at least for now. Camara stopped at one particular door and swiped a key card. It clicked to open and lights flickered on inside.

She waved them inside. "Welcome to my domain."

The unprepossessing exterior hid a cornucopia of academic delights and Martin's eyes widened as they walked in. The long room stretched back into the shadows with most of it separated off into temperature-controlled glass areas with ancient manuscripts, maps and illustrated documents pinned down for study.

An oversized teak desk covered with folders, loose papers

and books, some open with pages marked, nestled in a cozy alcove near the door. An Iranian samovar stood on a side table, a copper vessel used to boil water and prepare tea. This one was a mix of ancient and modern as it was plugged into an electric socket, constantly providing the sustenance that every academic needed. Martin smiled at how the office was laid out as it echoed his own world. Camara was perfectly put together in her lab and her physical appearance, but her desk betrayed a riotous intelligence behind closed doors, one that could not be tamed so easily by the expectations of others.

Flowering plants in rich vibrant colors surrounded the desk and above them, a wall of maps from different eras — all depicting the Middle East.

Camara led them over to the wall and pointed to one map that showed several pins dotted around a specific area. "These are some dig sites I've been researching, and this is the one where things were disrupted. I think Eden might be near here."

CHAPTER 12

THE LIBRARY WAS IN downtown Kingston, an unremarkable building with three stories of concrete and louvered windows, a relic of the 1970s. But sometimes, it was the non-descript buildings that held the most interesting objects. Jamaica had not digitally archived all their treasures, so this was the only way they could truly investigate the thread that Martin's database had discovered — a link between the Jews of Amsterdam and the pirates of Port Royal in the seventeenth century.

A tall, slender Jamaican woman greeted them at the door. She wore a professional trouser suit in dolphin grey with an ivory shirt beneath, the very model of a senior librarian. But as she reached out her hand to welcome them, Morgan noticed a tattoo on her wrist, a string of numbers running up her sleeve in the beginnings of a Dewey Decimal number.

"Welcome to the island. I'm Kimelia Washington, Head Librarian here at Jamaica's National Library."

Kimelia led Morgan and Jake into the main reading room. Students sat at long tables researching from books with broken spines, an old photocopier whirred in the corner, and a fan rotated slowly overhead. It didn't have the ancient beauty of some of the libraries of Europe, but Morgan recognized a love for knowledge in those present. A common thread that bound bibliophiles the world over.

"I believe you wanted to see William Jackson's journal from 1643?" Kimelia whispered.

Morgan nodded, respecting the quiet.

Kimelia led them on through the reading room and down a staircase lit by dim bulbs. "We keep the older documents away from sunlight and we can control the temperature more easily down here."

She opened a door at the bottom of the staircase, and they emerged into a storage area. Rows of shelves stacked with leather-bound ledgers of land deeds, tax records and business transactions stood next to boxes of documents, each marked with precise tiny writing.

Kimelia pulled down a box from the stack. "William Jackson was an English privateer. He captured Spanish ships and 'liberated' the cargo for England. In 1643, he anchored at Port Royal and led a successful raid on Spanish Town. Port Royal was notorious at the time, a haven for privateers and pirates."

She placed the box on the table, pulled white gloves from her pocket and put them on, before carefully reaching into the box and lifting out an old leather-bound book.

"This is his journal, but as you can see, it's difficult to decipher."

Morgan gazed down at the elaborate handwriting, a scrawl that would take even Martin's algorithms some time to translate. "We're looking for any mention of the Portuguese Jews."

Kimelia brightened. "You're in luck. I helped an author research this not long ago." She carefully turned the pages to a particular diary entry, the dark lines slightly faded with ink spots dotting the edges, and read a passage aloud. "Jamaica's capital was deserted except for diverse Portuguese of the Hebrew nation who came unto us seeking asylum and promised to show us where the Spaniards hid their gold."

Kimelia turned from the book and went to a large bookcase, pulling down a folio with loose maps. She selected a print. "An earthquake and a subsequent tsunami destroyed

Port Royal in 1692, but this painting from *National Geographic* has a depiction of what it might have looked like." She pointed to one area. "This was apparently a synagogue near the courthouse. There are also tombstones from the time with Hebrew writing alongside Portuguese. As experienced traders, the Jews were an important part of the Port Royal community."

Jake raised a questioning eyebrow. "So, there really were Jewish pirates?"

Kimelia nodded. "Yes, even a couple of famous ones. Sinan, Barbarossa's second-in-command, was referred to as 'the great Jewish pirate' in correspondence with Henry VII of England. The founders of the Amsterdam Jewish community, Samuel and Joseph Palache, were also originally pirates. They carved a phoenix on the bow of their ship, the bird that rises from the flames, who cannot be burned, representing the faith of the Jews that would always rise again from the fires of the Inquisition."

Morgan thought back to Rabbi Cohen on the edge of the pyre in Amsterdam, when he had looked like he would walk over the embers to the lost manuscripts buried beneath. The Jews of the Diaspora were a hardy bunch indeed, but it was hard to reconcile what she knew of bookish scholars like her father with the archetype of pirates brandishing cutlasses and hijacking treasure ships.

"They also acted as spies for the enemies of Spain," Kimelia continued. "Oliver Cromwell said that the Jews were good and useful spies when they assisted Britain in the conquest of Jamaica. They even sent word to Queen Elizabeth that the Armada was sailing."

"But how did the Jews come to be here?" Jake asked.

"Many came from Recife in Brazil." Kimelia pulled out an older map showing trade routes from South America into the Caribbean. "The Portuguese settled in what became known as Brazil in the mid-1500s and the Jews kept their faith a secret. But when the Dutch took some of the north-ern region and founded New Holland as a base for the West India Company in 1630, Jews were allowed to practice their faith openly."

Morgan imagined the freedom that suddenly opened up for people, and it made her smile to imagine them finally saying their prayers aloud.

"But it didn't last long," Kimelia continued. "The Spanish recaptured Recife in 1654 and the Jews left along with the Dutch. Some went to New Amsterdam which eventually became New York, some returned to Dutch Amsterdam and others sailed here to the Caribbean. They were successful traders and by the 1660s, there were Jewish settlements across the islands."

"Do you have any other documents from the time?" Morgan asked, walking over to look at the boxes more closely. They seemed to contain only land deeds and other historical documents, but she knew how much could be hidden. Books inside books, manuscripts inside tax records. The fragment of a map could be concealed anywhere.

Kimelia nodded. "Of course, what are you looking for in particular?"

"A fragment of an illustrated manuscript, part of a map. It might have plants on it or a tree and maybe some words in Hebrew."

Kimelia shook her head. "I've seen nothing like that and we have no illustrated works of that kind, but the Shaare Shalom Synagogue has an archive of Jewish material. It's just a few blocks from here."

* * *

Bright sun glared off the stark white exterior of the Shaare Shalom Synagogue as Morgan and Jake walked inside its gates. They passed palm trees and a well-watered garden as they headed toward the giant door.

It opened on their approach and an elderly black man walked out, wrinkles belying his age even though he moved with the sprightly ease of a younger man. He wore a *kippah* over his close-cropped white hair and beamed in welcome, holding out his arms wide. "Shalom, friends. I'm Desomond. Come on in."

The synagogue had two levels of dark wooden seating either side of a central area where the Torah Ark stood on a raised dais. There was sand on the floor, echoing Ets Haim in Amsterdam.

Desomond noticed Morgan glance down and explained the custom. "It's not a memento of the island's beaches as some think. It's to remind worshippers of the sand used to muffle footsteps back in the days of the Inquisition when we hid our faith. Others say that until we are back in Jerusalem, we must walk through the desert." He grinned. "But maybe it's just to keep out the snakes and insects."

He led them on to a less formal area for community events with plenty of plastic chairs, children's art and pictures of local festivities.

"We're a Reform synagogue with prayers in Hebrew and English and we encourage people of other faiths to visit. The more we understand each other, the more we can live together in peace."

Desomond stopped in front of a board of pictures and pointed to an image of a black man in glasses and a skullcap shaking hands with a Rabbi. "That's Louis Farrakhan, the leader of the Nation of Islam. He came here in 2002 in his first ever visit to a synagogue in an attempt to rebuild his relationships with Jews."

Jake pointed to a colorful picture, a group of people singing together against the backdrop of the white synagogue. Some had long dreadlocks tied back with green, yellow and red bands, others tucked their hair away in *tams*, round crocheted caps.

Desomond smiled. "That's a Nyabinghi we had here in 2012, a gathering of Rastafari people. They are not so far from the Jews, you know, singing songs of freedom in a strange land. Their Zion is Africa, and ours is Israel." He looked off into the distance. "Funny though, most of us have never been there. This is our home."

He led them on. "So I understand from Kimelia that you want to see the museum?"

Morgan nodded. "Yes, and in particular, any documents or fragments that might have been brought here by the Jews who came from Recife or even Portugal originally."

Desomond nodded. "We have some manuscripts stored in the archive. Have a look around and I'll go get them for you." He pushed open the doors of the museum and waved them inside with a smile. "I'll be back soon."

Jake walked over to the nearest display case, which contained several open prayer books. He bent to look more closely while Morgan walked to the back of the room. She noticed something, an illustration of some kind, in one of the glass cases.

But as she walked closer, she could see it was a map of Jamaica illustrated by a local artist. Beautiful, but not what they sought.

The sound of rapid footsteps came from the corridor.

Jake spun around, his expression alert. "What—?"

Morgan instinctively ducked down behind an exhibit, her years of training in the Israel Defense Force serving her well. She crouched low and peered around the corner of a cabinet.

The door to the museum burst open.

Desomond strode in, a pistol held out in front of him. Three scowling young men rushed in behind him, two with guns and one with a machete. Desomond was no longer the smiling custodian.

His face contorted with anger as he looked around the room. "Where's the woman?"

Jake didn't miss a beat. "She went to the bathroom. What is this? What's going on?"

One man slipped out to check.

Desomond brandished his gun. "You pursue a dangerous goal and your actions risk us all. There's a curse on that piece of manuscript and as I am a servant of the Lord, I cannot let you take it, no matter your credentials."

He motioned to the men, and they walked toward Jake with menace.

As they advanced, Morgan crawled silently around the back of the museum and slipped out the door into the garden.

In the reflection on the shiny wood, she could just glimpse Jake roughly pushed out through the main doors.

A shout came from the women's bathroom. "She's not here!"

Morgan ran.

She sprinted across the small garden and vaulted over the fence, landing heavily in a dusty backyard.

A dog started barking. The men would not be far behind.

Morgan rolled to her feet and ran again, out to the road and into the warren of streets around the synagogue. She stood out here as a white woman and they would find her trail soon enough. She had to get back to help Jake, but right now, she needed sanctuary in a strange city.

The library.

Kimelia's passion for history and her edgy tattoo made Morgan trust her. She would not have sent them to the synagogue if she'd known of what they sought or Desomond's clear relationship to the criminal side of Kingston.

Decision made, Morgan darted off through the streets.

* * *

The vicious kick glanced off his injured ribs and Jake let the wave of pain wash over him as he lay curled on the floor. He was no stranger to a beating, but he'd had a few too many lately. At least this man was an amateur, which gave Jake some hope. The blows were enthusiastic but not well-executed, and from what he'd heard about some criminal gangs in Jamaica, he could be in a lot more trouble right now.

At least Morgan had made it out. Two of the men had gone after her, leaving him with one young man and Desomond, who stood in the corner watching the beating with narrowed eyes.

They were in a concrete room in the basement of a house only a few blocks from the synagogue, definitely soundproof and clearly used for this kind of 'discussion,' judging by the blood spots on the floor. There were two chairs and a single bare bulb dangling above, lighting the room with a harsh glare.

The young man gave a last kick, then dragged Jake up and onto a chair, securing his hands behind him with a cable tie.

Desomond stepped forward. "What do you want with the Eden manuscript?"

Jake took a shallow breath, drawing air into his lungs with a painful wheeze. There seemed little point in lying, especially as the map fragment seemed to be close.

"We're trying to get to the pieces before someone else finds them first. Someone who uses fire and dynamite and murder to reach their goal."

Desomond frowned. "Why now? The pieces have been hidden for generations."

Jake explained about the attack on the Ets Haim Synagogue in Amsterdam and their journey to Lisbon and Macau, as well as their run-in with Frik Versfeld.

Desomond paced back and forward, his shoulders slumping more as he learned of the stolen pieces until he finally turned to the young man. "Go, I don't need you anymore."

The fighter looked disappointed and gave Jake a hard look before walking out.

Desomond wrung his hands together and wiped sweat from his brow. "I heard about Ets Haim. We thought it was an anti-Semitic attack, unfortunately common enough."

"What do you know of the fragments?" Jake asked. "Perhaps we can help each other?"

Desomond pulled the other chair across the room and sat opposite Jake. "There have been protectors of the piece for generations, tasked with making sure that no one ever puts the whole thing back together. To be honest, I've always doubted that the map was real. After all, Eden cannot possibly exist and even if there was once a garden, how could that be a danger to us now?" He shrugged. "But there is much about my faith that I don't understand, so I didn't question this task. No one ever asked about it until you arrived. That's why I reacted as I did."

Jake tugged at his bonds. "Any chance you want to take these off me? And maybe tell your men to go easy on my partner?"

Desomond narrowed his eyes. "Not so fast, my friend."

* * *

Morgan jogged along the street, staying the shadows. A blue sedan sped past, then shrieked to a halt in the road just meters away.

They had found her.

Morgan turned and ran down an alley. She was only a block from the library now. She might just make it.

Footsteps pounded the pavement behind her. It was only one man — but he was getting closer.

People walked the surrounding streets, but none paid any heed. This was an area of town where it was better not to witness anything untoward.

Just as Morgan reached the middle of the alley, the blue sedan pulled across the end, blocking her in. She looked around quickly, assessing the scene. Three metal dustbins surrounded by bags of rubbish. Discarded boxes. Not much else.

The man sprinted into the alley and stopped a few meters away. He was short but all meaty muscle, his t-shirt stretched tight against bulging biceps.

A wide smile spread across his face as he saw she was cornered. "If you come with us now, you won't get hurt — I promise."

His eyes said something different.

Morgan took a step back, shifting her weight and raising her hands with open palms in the Krav Maga fighting stance. She smiled back. "If you leave me alone, you won't get hurt — I promise."

He walked toward her with a confident swagger born from always being the bigger man, always being the dominant one in a fight.

Morgan let him come.

He grabbed for her shoulders with both hands.

She stepped back with her right leg, thrusting her arms up between his hands with crossed wrists —

Thrust her arms apart in a twisting motion, driving his arms away —

His eyes widened in surprise.

She slammed her flat palms over his ears to stun him, stepped forward, and drove her knee into his groin.

It was over in a few seconds. Just as it should be.

The big man doubled over, hands wrapped around his head as he rolled to the ground.

As Morgan sprinted away, she heard the blue sedan rev up. It wouldn't be far behind.

*   *   *

Desomond glared at Jake. "Tell me why you're chasing after the map. Why should I give you the fragment?"

"I'm with an organization called ARKANE. We find and protect precious religious artifacts — amongst other things. We have a vault in London, where the pieces can be safe."

The old man shook his head. "They've been safe for generations by keeping them apart."

Jake shifted in his chair to ease the pressure on his bruised ribs. "That may be, but now someone wants to find Eden and they will stop at nothing to bring the pieces together."

Desomond sagged in his chair and suddenly looked older than his years.

"The elder who passed this sacred task to me died decades ago. I'm the only one who knows of the fragment here in Jamaica. To be honest, there's no one I can pass it on to. The community is small and every year that goes by, I worry that I will die with the knowledge."

"Let me help you," Jake said softly. "We found this place, so others after the fragment will come soon. They may already be on the island. If we take the piece now, you and the community will be safe."

"It will only be safe once you're gone." Desomond stood up and pulled a penknife from his pocket, flicking open the sharp blade.

CHAPTER 13

Desomond walked around the back of the chair and cut through the cable tie. Jake massaged his wrists to get the circulation moving again and stood up to stretch.

Desomond sheepishly indicated Jake's shirt, now covered with dust and dirty footprints from the beating. "I'm sorry about all this."

Jake gingerly felt around his ribs. Not too much worse than before, but then he knew how to protect himself even on the ground. "It's OK. Your guy clearly needed the practice."

He thought of Frik back in the burning church on Macau. These amateurs were lucky that they picked on the right South African. "Can you call off the men looking for Morgan?"

A flash of concern crossed Desomond's face. "Of course. Come. We'll return to the synagogue. You should tell her to meet us back there."

As soon as they got outside, Jake called Morgan. The phone rang and rang before she eventually picked up, her breath ragged.

"You alright?" she asked, her voice more concerned for him than her own safety.

He should have known she'd be fine. Sometimes, Jake wished he could help his partner more, but Morgan had a core of strength that he couldn't even find in himself some days. After all, he was the one beaten to the ground, and she was out running around the city.

"I'm fine." Jake glanced over at Desomond. "Just a misunderstanding. Can you come back to the synagogue?"

"On my way."

* * *

Morgan turned from the call to see the blue sedan pulling up across the street. This time she stood her ground.

The man she had beaten looked out the window, his face mottled with rage. He mouthed some swear words at her, recognizable in any language, but clearly they'd been told to leave her alone. The driver pulled away.

She turned and jogged back to the synagogue. Whatever Jake had done, he'd managed to turn the situation around, whereas she'd resorted to violence. Morgan wished she had the even temper and sense of humor that Jake brought to every mission, despite the dire circumstances they sometimes found themselves in. She was lucky to have him as a partner. They complemented each other's abilities — most of the time, at least — and he watched her back as she watched his. This time, though, she worried about his personal history with the hitman, Frik Versfeld. Would their shared past jeopardize the mission?

She rounded one last corner to find Desomond standing just inside the gates of the synagogue, Jake sitting on an ornate bench beside him. Her partner looked a little green, and he clutched his ribs over a dirty shirt. He hadn't escaped completely unscathed.

Jake stood up when he saw her, his hands dropping from his rib cage. She smiled at his attempt to hide his pain, but they had worked together long enough that she knew his tells. The tightening of the corkscrew scar at his temple, the tension in his jaw, the way he moved in a slightly jolted fashion.

"Desomond's got something to show us," he said.

Morgan smiled. "About time."

The old man led them into the museum, and this time, he didn't hesitate. He opened a large sea chest at the back of the room and pulled out several knitted blankets, a pile of baby clothes, and what looked like lost property from the community. A ragtag collection of unwanted objects and underneath it all, a small metal safe.

Desomond pulled it out with a haunted look in his eyes. "Jake has convinced me that this will be safer with you."

He placed it on one of the display cabinets and entered the combination. The safe swung open to reveal a small glass case. Desomond put his hand inside and rested it on the fragment.

He looked up at Jake. "I'm entrusting you with my sacred duty. The Lord knows I've carried it long enough." He pulled out the glass case and looked down at its muted colors. "You must not let the pieces touch one another again. The risk is too great. Humanity was expelled from Eden for a reason, and we must never try to return there."

Jake nodded. "I'll keep it close to me."

Morgan noted that he did not actually promise anything, and for that, she was grateful. This Jewish community had such a rich history and traced its lineage back to Brazil, to Portugal, and to Amsterdam. She wanted to honor their origins, but they still needed to find the next piece.

She bent to look at the fragment in Jake's hand. It showed four rivers swirling around a Hebrew word. *Arar.*

Cursed.

A sense of foreboding rose within her as she examined the ancient writing, but she pushed it aside. "Do you know the origins of this piece? Which community did it come from originally?"

Desomond nodded. "It's from Recife in Brazil."

* * *

Paris, France

Camara pointed to a mountainous area east of the Tigris in the governorate of Nineveh. Sebastian bent to look more closely until his cheek almost brushed against hers. The professor didn't move away and for a moment, Martin thought perhaps he should leave them alone to catch up.

A second later, Camara stepped away, her face slightly flushed.

She switched on the samovar and as the water boiled, she gathered three tiny glasses and placed a sugar cube at the bottom of each. "If we're going to talk about the Middle East, then let's do it with traditional hospitality."

As she siphoned the tea from the samovar, the smell of mint and herbs filled the air. Martin took a sip of the dark green liquid, grateful for the sugar as it tasted like some kind of foul medicine. Sebastian drank it without comment, so Martin sipped at his glass, determined to give it a try.

Camara placed her tea down to cool a little before drinking while she shuffled aside some books on her desk until she found a particular one. A battered copy of the Bible in French, its brown leather cover soft from use over generations.

"The location of Eden is complicated by the names of the rivers in the book of Genesis, chapter two." She opened the Bible and translated for them. "'A river flows out of Eden to water the garden, and from there it divides and becomes four branches.' The Pishon, the Gihon, the Tigris and the Euphrates."

"So we just trace the path of the rivers, right?" Martin followed the Tigris on the map from the mountains of south-eastern Turkey through to the Persian Gulf, and then the path of the Euphrates to the west. Together they framed the ancient land of Mesopotamia, the land between the rivers, now modern Iraq, Kuwait, and eastern parts of Syria and Turkey. He frowned. "Where are the Pishon and the Gihon?"

Camara smiled at his dawning realization. "Exactly. That's where scholars differ in their interpretation."

Martin turned from the map. "Can it be discerned from historical documents?"

"Many have tried, and all have failed." Camara put down the Bible and pulled an oversized tome from a shelf behind her desk, a folio of maps and documents collected over a lifetime of study. She opened it to a black and white print of a *mappa mundi*, a holy map of the world from the Middle Ages.

"There are different ideas. The Jewish historian, Josephus, identified the 'land of Cush' that borders Eden in Genesis with the African kingdom of Kush, south of Egypt. A twelfth-century theologian, Honorius of Autun, writes of the four rivers going underground in Asia then surfacing far away, the Gihon as the Nile, the Pishon as the Ganges."

Martin frowned. "But Eden would need to be at the source of all four and that's geographically impossible."

Sebastian finished the last of his tea, put down the glass and pointed at the map on the wall. "What about Armenia? If you follow the rivers back, they could start in the southern slopes of the Taurus Mountains and split into four streams lower down."

Camara nodded. "That possibility is favored by some scholars." She paged through the folio to a map of a verdant green paradise. "Others have suggested the source is Mount Amara in Ethiopia. The word *amara* means paradise in the Ethiopian language and the area is abundant with fruit trees and has year-round sun and rain. It featured in Milton's *Paradise Lost*, although Milton himself located Eden in Assyria."

She turned another page to a photocopy of scrawled, spidery handwriting. "Then there are the words of Christopher Columbus, who claimed to have found the four rivers emptying from the Orinoco River into the Gulf of Paria just off modern-day Venezuela. A rugged mountain rose above it with an unreachable summit. He said, 'If this river does not flow out of the earthly Paradise, the marvel is still greater. For I do not believe that there is so great and deep a river anywhere in the world.'"

Martin shook his head. "All these possible places. If there's evidence for so many, how are we meant to find the most likely location?"

As he looked at the image, the map undulated, the green expanding and contracting like some kind of mutant lung. He felt a little woozy and placed a hand on the wall to steady himself.

Sebastian sighed. "Or is Eden just an allegory? Was there ever really a physical garden?" He leaned against the wall, his body sagging as if he had reached the end of his energy reserves.

Camara lifted her glass of tea and turned to one last page. "If you think of Eden as an actual garden, the same one that bloomed at the beginning of time, it cannot possibly be true. But I am of the same mind as John Calvin, who included this map in his commentary on Genesis and put it east of Babylon. The Gihon was the western branch of the Euphrates and the Pishon the southern branch of the Tigris."

She took a sip of the tea and grimaced. "This tastes strange. Did you…?"

Camara's voice faded as the world dimmed. Martin's vision narrowed to the lines on the wall in front of him. He fell to the floor, his limbs immobile, his skin clammy, his mouth dry. The last thing he saw was Camara's terror as she ran to help.

* * *

Camara bent over Sebastian's prone form and tugged at his shoulders to turn him onto his side in the recovery position in case he vomited. His face was pale and a cold sweat formed on his brow. His breath was fast and ragged. His colleague, Martin, lay on his side with the same affliction.

The tea. Someone had doctored it — but with what?

She had only taken a sip of the bitter brew, but both men had drunk a full glass. It could be any number of poisons, and many dangerous plants were even grown here in the lab. Possibilities ran quickly through her mind, a litany of toxins and their terrible effects. Although her life's work revolved around the wonders of botany, Camara understood that Nature was not her friend.

Now it might kill the only man she had ever loved.

Despite his betrayal all those years ago, Camara couldn't help the rush of excitement that flooded her as Sebastian had stood in the library. The years had marked them both, but she still saw glimpses of the man she had known underneath. She would not let him go so easily this time.

She reached for her office phone to call the emergency services. It was dead. Not even a dial tone. She grabbed her mobile. The network was gone. Something blocked it.

Camara darted to her office door —

It opened before she could reach it.

A young man stepped inside, dark curls cropped close to his skull with a neatly trimmed beard and mustache. He wore a t-shirt of a local band and jeans that stretched over a muscled torso. Just a student she had never seen before.

"Please, help me," Camara said. "We need to call an ambulance. My phones aren't working."

But as the young man closed the door behind him, he looked at her with the intensity of a fanatic. She'd made a terrible mistake.

Camara opened her mouth to scream.

The stranger stepped quickly over the bodies of the prone men and pushed her against the desk, one cool hand over her mouth.

She struggled, fighting his iron grip, desperate to get away, as he wrestled her slight frame into submission.

A prick of a needle on her neck.

As cold spread throughout her body in a chill paralysis, Camara's last thought was of Sebastian. How could she have found him once more only to lose him again so soon?

*   *   *

Guram gently laid the professor down on the floor, resting her head on one of her many books. It was important to keep her in a good condition. She needed to be perfect when she entered the Garden. A flawless sacrifice.

He looked down at the bodies of the two men. The professor's next appointment was only minutes away, so he didn't have enough time to deal with them properly. Guram dragged them behind the huge desk. They would be found, but not immediately, and by then, it would be too late.

He went inside one of the glass labs and wheeled out a trolley used to transport samples and equipment. It was easy enough to fold the professor's petite frame into the bottom and cover her with a tarpaulin before placing several small bushes on top.

Guram opened the door and wheeled the trolley out into the busy corridors. No one gave him a second glance as he pushed his precious cargo out into the loading dock at the back of the building.

Brother Hadiq stood tapping his foot nervously at the rear of a van, the doors open and ready to go. Guram wheeled the trolley up the ramp and into the back, securing it for the journey ahead. Brother Hadiq closed the doors behind him, slamming them shut with a sound of finality.

CHAPTER 14

Recife, Brazil

Jake received a text message as the plane began to circle in descent. The buzzing woke Morgan from a light sleep and she turned to see his expression darken as he read.

"What is it?"

Jake bit his lip, knuckles tightening around his phone as he summarized the message. "Professor Camara Mbaye has been kidnapped from her lab in Paris. Martin and Sebastian were drugged but they're recovering."

Morgan sat up, her mind whirling as she processed the news. Once again, ARKANE had endangered those who should be safe, and after what happened to Ines, it was surely only a matter of time before they heard more bad news.

She shifted a little to loosen her muscles. They'd been on way too many flights in the last few days. "You think it was Frik?"

Jake frowned. "It's not really his style. Not enough obvious destruction." He continued to read from the message. "Security cameras show a young man wheeling a trolley out of Professor Mbaye's office to a van. ARKANE's preliminary analysis matched him with photos provided by Turkish intelligence. He's connected to an agricultural complex in the east of Turkey owned by a holding company suspected to be part of a disavowed Catholic Order of monks, the Ignis Flammae."

"The flaming sword," Morgan said. "Genesis, chapter three says that God placed 'cherubim and a flaming sword flashing back and forth to guard the way to the tree of life.' Metaphors perhaps, symbols, or—"

"Something altogether more real," Jake finished for her. "If this Order have taken the professor, it implies she knows too much about the location of Eden."

Morgan gazed out the window to the edge of the city below as the plane banked over the Atlantic Ocean. "Then if we find the Garden, we'll find the professor. We have to locate the next piece as fast as we can."

* * *

The taxi crawled from the airport into the city of Recife through dense traffic, apparently normal enough as the chatty taxi driver informed them. Morgan tuned him out and watched the world go by.

These moments of movement between locations were a welcome pause, enforced time when they could do nothing. Their missions focused on action, always taking the next step, but it was in these pauses that both she and Jake did a lot of their thinking. This assignment had many puzzling aspects, and the professor's abduction by a mysterious Order added a new dimension. If the monks went to such lengths to keep it hidden, perhaps the Garden was real after all.

The taxi finally reached the inner city. Sprawling skyscrapers reflected a thriving modern culture, and the architecture of the Old Town had elements that reminded Morgan of Lisbon. European-style facades in rich colors of mustard yellow, sky blue and peach with white trim, and decorative archways leading to spacious plazas.

Recife was sometimes called the Venice of Brazil for its waterways, rivers and bridges, but most tourists headed for the adjoining community of Olinda, a UNESCO World Heritage Site with preserved colonial architecture, winding stone streets and picturesque churches. While Morgan wished they had time to stop for a *caipirinha* overlooking the ocean, time ticked away and Professor Mbaye's abduction remained at the forefront of her mind.

The taxi driver dropped them on the Praça do Marco Zero, an open square with a colorful mosaic pavement popular with locals for promenading and street entertainment. With views out to the reefs that gave the city its name, it hosted a market with local produce and artisan goods. As Jake paid the driver, a trickle of sweat ran down Morgan's spine in the intense humidity, the air heavy even here on the coast.

They meandered along the edge of the plaza, enjoying the lively atmosphere as the beat of the *maracatu* drums drifted across the hubbub of the market. The enticing smell of smoky barbecue meat, the tang of citrus, and sweet chocolate with a hint of chili hung in the air.

As they passed the edge of the stalls, Morgan noticed an old woman sitting on a blanket behind rows of pottery figurines, each set representing different aspects of Brazilian history. There were Portuguese explorers, a native tribal group and a modern Carnival parade. One portrayed a group of black men joined in a slave gang, arms chained together, their faces carefully etched in suffering.

Morgan had been surprised to find out about the history of the slave trade from Martin's notes about the country. Brazil was initially named Terra de Vera Cruz, Land of the True Cross, and it seemed incredible that such a tiny state as Portugal could claim a land as large as Western Europe. There were so many riches to harvest and yet, the Portuguese did not have enough people to colonize and do the work.

So they brought slaves.

Over three hundred years, the Portuguese transported

four million slaves from Africa to Brazil in what some considered to be the largest forced migration in history, ten times the number taken to North America by other countries. The slaves worked the gold and diamond mines as well as sugar plantations, cattle ranches and coffee fields. Brazil was the last country in the Western world to abolish slavery in 1888, many years after England in 1807 and the US in 1865. Racial tensions and socio-economic inequality still remained in the country today.

As Morgan bent to examine the pottery figures more closely, the rhythmic beat of percussion drifted across the square. Jake walked toward the sound and joined a gathering circle. Morgan went to stand with him, watching as a group of young people warmed up with flowing movements.

Musicians began to play on one edge of the circle. One held a *berimbau*, a single-stringed percussion instrument with a gourd at the bottom, another tapped on the *pandeiro* hand drum while two more sat with larger wooden *atabaque* drums. As they struck up a rhythm, two of the young people moved opposite each other in low rocking steps, as others clapped and sang around them.

As the music speeded up, the movements became more aggressive with rolling and sweeping, spinning kicks and cartwheels. Somehow, the pair avoided touching even though their limbs passed within millimeters of each other in graceful acrobatic moves.

"It's *capoeira*," Jake explained. "A martial art developed here in Brazil by enslaved Africans. They practiced it like a dance or a game to avoid detection, but it could also be used to defend themselves."

As the *capoeiristas* finished playing, the crowd erupted with applause. Morgan and Jake weaved their way back through the crowd and into the streets behind the plaza, eventually emerging outside the modest Kahal Zur Israel. With its cream facade and terracotta-red shutters, it looked like any other building on the block except for the prominent name on the side.

Sinagoga Kahal Zur Israel had been established in 1636, the first synagogue erected in the Americas, even though Jews had been living in Brazil since the Portuguese arrived in 1500. Recife was the first slave port in the Americas and experienced a rare period of religious freedom when the Dutch took the city between 1630 and 1654 — but it didn't last long.

When Portugal reconquered the area, many of the Jews left, some heading for Amsterdam in Holland, some for New Amsterdam, later called New York, and others for Jamaica, where Port Royal fell under British protection. Morgan marveled at how the routes of the Diaspora wove their way back and forth across the world, following trade and religious freedom, tying cultures together in unusual ways. This intermingling was both a blessing and a curse, a way for people to understand those they considered 'Other,' but also provoking conflict.

Jake knocked at the door of the synagogue and a homely woman opened it, her ample curves hidden under an oversized t-shirt and jeans, her gaze piercingly intelligent.

"I'm Fernanda," she said warmly. "Custodian of the synagogue museum. Desomond called me to vouch for you both. Our congregations are linked on some Jewish Diaspora online communities and he and I share an interest in ancient manuscripts." She raised an eyebrow. "I hear we have that interest in common?"

Jake nodded and pulled the fragment encased in glass from his pack. "We're looking for something similar to this."

Fernanda took it from him and inspected it with the enthusiasm of a scholar. A moment later, she frowned and gave it back, taking a step away as if it held some terrible disease.

"You recognize the curse?" Morgan asked.

Fernanda shook her head. "It's not that." She sighed. "We have something similar and it marks a dark time in our history. Come. I'll show you."

She led them through the synagogue. It was stark with plain timber flooring, hard wooden benches, and stone walls, a functional house of worship designed to keep the place cool. The museum section beyond was well laid-out with informative panels about Portuguese Jewish history, and ritual objects in glass cases.

Fernanda stopped at a nondescript door at the end of the gallery. "This leads to another museum, accessible to the public through a different entrance. We like to keep some separation. It's no good to dwell on the past, but this is truly a cruel history."

She pushed open the door into the Museu da História da Inquisição, the Museum of the History of the Inquisition. As they stepped over the threshold, Morgan felt a sense of heaviness descend, as if the very air thickened around her. She understood why the synagogue would want to keep this place separate. It was important to remember, but the past did not define everything about the present and the Jewish community thrived in the Diaspora now, despite every attempt to stamp them out.

"New Christians, also known as Esperandos, Hopeful Ones, came to Brazil, seeking a new life," Fernanda explained as she led them through the gallery. "They became traders and shipowners, a merchant class who set up sugar factories and cultivated tea and coffee plantations. They traded with New Christians on the Iberian Peninsula and later with Amsterdam and London. But the Jews were not safe in the New World either. The Inquisition arrived in 1591, their primary role to seek out the New Christians who hid their true faith, and forcibly convert any Jews who dared to live openly. Many people have heard of the violent excesses of the Spanish Inquisition but the Portuguese were just as bad."

They walked past panels with historical information and engravings of torture and broken bodies burning at the stake. A list of names etched into marble hung on the wall nearby, dedicated to the victims of the Jewish Inquisition. Yosef Bemvenist, Isaque Gabal, Moseh de Azeuedo, and so many more.

Morgan recited the names in her mind, sounding out the syllables of lives ended in agony. The screams and the crackle of flames had been silenced by the years but still resonated in the memories of those who remained.

A plain wooden table made of thick planks stood in the middle of one room with shackles at either end to hold a body down, and a central winding handle to stretch the victim. At the foot of the rack, a double-ended saw with wicked teeth, next to neck screws and blades for flaying flesh. Just a few of the replica torture instruments held in the museum.

"The Inquisition was finally abolished in Brazil in 1824." Fernanda shook her head. "It's hard to believe that they dominated for several hundred years of misery. Of course, anti-Semitism has not gone away, but at least we don't face the auto-da-fé anymore."

"You said you recognized the fragment?" Jake said, a gentle attempt to bring the conversation back to their mission.

Morgan understood the need for haste, but part of her wanted to learn more about the Jews of this part of the world. Her own heritage was Sephardic with the Sierra family part of the Spanish Diaspora. Her father had been a Kabbalah scholar, always fascinated by history. She imagined his enthusiasm for learning about something new, and a little of the heaviness lifted as she thought of his smiling face. He had passed on like all these dead around her, but a part of them lived on in their descendants. So it had always been. So it would ever be.

Fernanda walked on into a small annex off the main gallery. "We keep documents here."

Hand-written letters in white frames lined the walls alongside tax and financial records written in Portuguese and Hebrew. A wide chest of drawers took up most of the space with a glass display case on top containing illustrations of Inquisition torture. Fernanda pulled open one drawer to reveal a manuscript fragment, the brown of the tree trunk faded to a light sepia, the surrounding text obscured by the grime of years. But the piece was recognizably part of the Eden map.

"That's it," Jake said. "Can we look at it more closely? Maybe borrow it for a while?"

Fernanda shook her head. "I'm sorry, but we don't let any of these items out of the museum. So much has been lost over the history of the Jews in Brazil, and we are now the sacred keepers of what's left. It is precious little, so I'm sure you can understand why I can't let you take it."

Her steely gaze matched the note of finality in her voice. There was no way they were taking the fragment.

CHAPTER 15

"OF COURSE." JAKE SMILED, but Morgan noticed that it didn't crinkle the corkscrew at the corner of his eyebrow. She knew his tells, but she couldn't see how they were going to get the fragment out of here and to be honest, Morgan wanted to respect the community's wishes. But if they left the fragment here, Frik Versfeld might come and take it — and he wouldn't be so polite. The community was not safe while it remained in the museum.

"Could we at least take some photographs?" she asked.

Fernanda nodded. "That would be fine." She pulled out the fragment and laid it on the glass.

Both Morgan and Jake took pictures on their phones from all kinds of different angles. It would have to be enough for now.

They had one physical piece and pictures of two more. That just left the final quarter, stolen by Frik in Macau. It might be enough, but then again, it might not be, and they were running out of time.

As they walked out of the synagogue, Morgan considered the photos Martin had sent previously. Aurelia dos Santos Fidalgo covertly photographed at an eco-terrorist event and evidence that the heiress had siphoned funds from the mining empire to those who wanted to destroy it. Despite their differences, they both sought a common goal. Perhaps together, they could find Eden — and rescue the professor.

It was time to reach out to their enemy.

* * *

En route to Turkey

Camara drifted in and out of unconsciousness, slowly becoming aware of a continuous droning sound and an occasional jolt beneath her. She could smell oil, the tang of metal and stale sweat. Her hands were bound in front, her legs tied together at the ankles, and as she opened her eyes, she realized that she was strapped to a side bench in a cargo plane surrounded by what looked like military equipment. She couldn't move.

Nausea rose within, her stomach spasming as the stink of the aircraft, her own fear and whatever drug the man had used mingled together in her system.

Sebastian.

Camara remembered how he had looked on the floor of her lab in those last moments, his dear face pale, a cold sweat on his skin. She could only hope that he and his colleague had been found soon enough. Sebastian had been tough in his youth, seemingly immune to the rigors of life in West Africa, but that was many years ago — and they weren't young anymore.

She didn't know what these people wanted, but it had to be about Eden. Perhaps she had located it correctly after all. Perhaps she would even see it before they… Camara pushed the dark thoughts aside. Whoever they were, they were keeping her alive for now, and that was something.

As the plane rocked a little, she closed her eyes again, retreating into the haven of memory.

It was a decade after independence, and Senegal was working out how to amplify its role in Africa while retaining links to the French Republic. Like much of colonial history throughout the continent, there had been atrocities and human rights abuses — but there had also been a positive side to its ties with the former ruling country. Camara had been a botanist at the University of Dakar in her first years of post-graduate study with a grant to research the survival aspects of plant species in the Sahel, a transitory region between the Sahara Desert and the savannah.

It had taken weeks to put together a support team and gather the right gear to survive in the harsh terrain. The day before they were due to leave, Camara repacked the Land Rover for the third time, checking items against her list once more. Could she possibly move things around to fit in a few more sample test tubes?

"Bonjour." The deep voice startled her, and Camara spun around, dropping her clipboard into the dust.

The man stepped forward and picked it up, his hand brushing hers as he handed it back. The sun caught his blonde hair, turning it to gold, and beneath his khaki shirt, Camara could see he was slim and tanned. His eyes were a piercing blue with a hint of mischief, and he had a lively smile.

"Forgive me for disturbing you, Miss Mbaye. I'm Sebastian Northbrook. I hear you're going into the Sahel?"

Camara nodded. "Yes, we leave tomorrow. Why do you ask?"

Sebastian pulled out a letter with the seal of the Senegalese Republic. "I'm researching the Wagadou, the ancient empire of Ghana, and you're going near the area I need to visit. Do you have room for one more?" He opened his jacket, indicating a fat wallet of West African francs. "I'm willing to pay and I have generous backers."

His money and his smile had been more than enough to convince Camara. She'd sourced a second vehicle with his cash, so they had more than enough room for her extra equipment, and she expanded her team to include another research assistant and driver. Sebastian joined them the next morning, a military pack on his back with his own gear, and they set off into the Sahel.

It was a magical time. Camara and her assistants gathered samples by day, working to understand the unique biogeographic realm and how plants survived in such a variable climate. Sebastian headed off every morning to photograph remote buried villages and catalogue stories from tribal elders.

In the evenings, they sat together by the fire, talking of their various discoveries. One night, after the others retired to their tents, Sebastian beckoned Camara to join him on the top of the Land Rover. The stars were bright diamonds in the velvet sky above, and he named the constellations in English while she told him the French words and some African tribal expressions.

When she shivered with the cold, he opened his jacket and with only a moment's hesitation, Camara moved into his arms. Their fingers entwined, their lips met, and as the stars of the southern hemisphere shone above, they both found something that transcended culture and history.

During that precious time in the Sahel, Camara was truly happy. They made the most of every moment, exploring the landscape by day and each other by night. She wished that time would stand still and they could stay far away from the city forever, but life moved on regardless and the research trip was soon over.

On the day they arrived back in Dakar, Sebastian went back to his lodgings, promising to visit her in the evening. When he returned far later than expected, he was distant and a little cold, his gaze fixed beyond her on the horizon. Then he kissed her and all was forgotten as she melted in his arms once more.

The next morning, Camara woke with the dawn and turned over, a lazy smile on her face, expecting to see Sebastian asleep beside her.

But he was gone.

She lay there for a while expecting him to walk back in the door with his aristocratic smile, a pot of fresh coffee in his hand. But when he did not return, Camara began to worry. There were many things that could befall an Englishman known to have money in the capital of Senegal.

By the time she made it to his lodgings, the sun was high overhead. The guesthouse manager looked at her with pity. Sebastian had left for the airport earlier, his final bill paid in full. There had been a letter from England waiting for him — perhaps that had been the catalyst for his departure.

Camara walked the streets of Dakar that day, exhausting herself as she tried to forget the way his laugh made her smile, how his blue eyes lit up at the sight of her, and how they had lain together under the moonlight.

How could she have ever thought it would last? He was a British aristocrat, heir to a fortune, and she was a poor Senegalese botanist. Their skin color was only a tiny part of their difference. One they didn't consider important — but others certainly did.

As the weeks went by, Camara hoped for a letter of explanation, but Sebastian never contacted her again. She channeled her anger into research, rapidly excelling in her field. She applied for every position that would enable her to leave Senegal and her old life behind, finally winning a place at the Hebrew University of Jerusalem in Israel to study paleo-botany. It was a junior role, but it was her way out and eventually, Camara made it to Paris, her dream even as a child.

She had searched for Sebastian later in life and discovered that his father had died while they were out in the Sahel. He had returned to take over custodianship of the John Soane Museum in London. Camara considered Sebastian's love of freedom, his passion for exploration, and she couldn't imagine that man tied down to some crumbling old institution

— but she also knew he deeply respected his father and the duties of family.

As her career progressed, there had been men in her life, and much love and happiness, but Camara had never forgotten those nights in the Sahel and the English aristocrat who made her feel like an African queen.

As the plane jolted beneath her, she thought of Sebastian as he now was, a fragile old man, and hoped that she would have a chance to see him once more.

* * *

Recife, Brazil

As Morgan phoned and left a message for Aurelia at the headquarters of the mining empire, Jake paced up and down on the edge of the busy plaza. The sound of samba drums and the *cavaquinho* guitar filled the air and a group of locals danced on the shore, laughing with the joy of movement amongst friends, bottles of cold Bohemia Weiss beer in their hands.

But Jake didn't feel like celebrating.

He stared out across the water to the reef beyond, where modern sculptures stood like sentinels against the wild ocean on the other side. The next stop east was Angola, Africa, once a Portuguese colony with one of the biggest slave ports. Only tiny Ascension Island lay in the thousands of miles between the continents, a British Overseas Territory maintained for strategic reasons in the middle of the Atlantic.

Jake found his thoughts as turbulent as the sea, tumbling with memory and regret. As much as he knew it made sense to try to make a deal with Aurelia dos Santos Fidalgo, he dreaded the thought of seeing Frik again and it seemed

J.F. PENN

impossible to think that the pair of them could put their differences aside and work together to find Eden.

He had made mistakes in his life, of course he had. No one lived without some form of regret, but Jake had tried to make up for the lives lost and damaged in the mining accident that scarred Frik. He had thought the balance tipped in his favor over the years by the massacres prevented, catastrophes averted, and destruction halted in his missions with ARKANE — and in truth, he hadn't thought of the mine in years. But Frik's fury gave him pause.

It was the butterfly effect in action. A tiny mis-judgment made, an angry word spoken instead of withheld, a decision taken in a moment of rage that led to a man pursuing a path of violence. Ripples spread out from each blow of a fist and slash of a blade until it was impossible to know how many lives had been impacted by his spur-of-the-moment decision long ago.

A shout rang out from one of the excited crowd and Jake turned to see the young people laughing together as they danced, couples holding hands, smiling and flirting. Their skin tones varied from light European descent, through the darker shades of those with indigenous ancestors to the black skin of those who could trace their blood to Africa. This country was the very definition of mixed race, the butterfly effect of hundreds of brutal decisions, the death and transplantation of millions — and yet, this cultural richness was the result and these young people were the hope of a positive future.

Jake couldn't change his past, just as Europeans could not wipe out the impact of historical colonization and slavery on the world. He could only move forward and try to make amends. Perhaps he and Frik could overcome their broken past and work together after all.

Morgan's phone buzzed with a message, and Jake hurried over to read the details with her.

Aurelia was willing to meet. They were going to Rio.

CHAPTER 16

Rio de Janeiro, Brazil

The helicopter swooped over the city toward the mountain topped by the gigantic statue of Christ the Redeemer, his outstretched arms welcoming all who visited.

Morgan gazed out the window at the packed streets below, the districts that led to the Rodrigo de Freitas Lagoon and the beaches of Ipanema and Copacabana on the edge of the Atlantic Ocean. She imagined diving beneath the cool water, letting the waves wash away thoughts of the mission and her worries about the missing professor, as well as Sebastian, still in recovery after the poisoning. She did not want another unnecessary death on her conscience.

They landed near the crest of the mountain, named Temptation Peak by the Portuguese when they arrived in the 1500s but now known as Corcovado for its resemblance to a hunchback. The wind picked up as Morgan and Jake emerged from the helicopter, a stiff breeze blowing in the scent of salt from the ocean and cedar wood from the Tijuca National Park below, the largest urban forest in the world.

A winding path took them up to the main viewing area, a series of concrete platforms around the towering statue of the Redeemer. A stunning view lay beyond in every direction — to the city, the beaches and the forest below.

It was still early, so there were only a few tourists around with no sign of Aurelia or her bodyguard. Morgan had some doubt as to whether they would even show up, and she and Jake were alert to the possibility that they might try to take the remaining piece by force. But time was running out, and this seemed like the only practical way forward.

Morgan walked to the railing and looked out across the Bay of Guanabara. Its hilly green islands sparkled in the morning sun, a light mist blowing across the peninsula like a veil over a mystical land.

"It's beautiful," she sighed. "I wish we had more time to…"

Her words trailed off as she turned back toward Jake. Behind him, only meters away, Aurelia dos Santos Fidalgo, the fine-boned heiress, stood with Frik Versfeld, his muscular frame seemingly even larger next to her diminutive size.

Jake spun around and Morgan put a hand on his arm to hold him back. She could sense his barely restrained desire to finish what Frik had started with Ines's death, and if she was honest, Morgan would be happy to help. But they needed those fragments, and she was willing to put aside their differences to achieve the greater goal. The living were more important than the dead.

Frik stared at Jake with a murderous gaze, his scarred neck flushed as he tamped down the rage that threatened to explode. But Aurelia smiled as she walked down the plaza steps, a look of serenity on her face as she approached, her bodyguard close by but clearly under orders to stay quiet.

"Welcome to my beautiful country." She opened her arms, echoing the Redeemer's pose high above her. Morgan considered that the heiress might well think of herself as some kind of saint, protecting Nature with her actions. Perhaps a modern day Francis of Assisi, who gave up his wealthy life to serve God, eventually becoming patron saint of animals and the natural environment.

"I'm glad you called," Aurelia said. "It seems our interests are aligned."

She walked to the edge of the viewing platform and stood within Morgan's reach. Frik stretched out a hand to stop the heiress from moving too close, but she held up one palm in a quick gesture, a clear direction to leave her alone. He remained alert a little further back, eyes flicking back and forth between Morgan and Jake, ready for any sudden movement.

Jake edged away from Morgan, splitting the bodyguard's attention even further. Aurelia continued, unaware of the unspoken power play between the three professionals around her.

"I've formally requested the fragment from the synagogue in Recife. The mayor was a dear friend of my late father and he is expediting the request. It will be here later today." She turned to Morgan. "So, I'd really like the piece of the map you found in Jamaica to complete my collection."

Aurelia exuded the entitlement of the ultra-rich, so used to people giving her what she wanted that she assumed no opposition to her goal. But Morgan had known many like her, especially in her years at the University of Oxford, and she would not be intimidated. She gave a half-smile. "What do you expect the map to give you that you don't already have?"

Aurelia pointed down at the forest below.

"These trees began their journey around three hundred million years ago, but humanity takes them for granted. Each leaf is a miracle of creation, and yet for all our architectural accomplishments, we still don't know how to construct something as perfect. We only how to destroy them."

She sighed. "Did you know that we've cut down over fifty billion trees in the last ten years? We are literally killing the natural world that sustains us, and in the process, we're killing ourselves. But Nature doesn't need us. In fact, She would be better off without our species. The map will lead us to Eden, and I believe something there will tip the balance in Her favor. It's time to end the Anthropocene, the age of humans."

Aurelia spoke emphatically with seemingly no sense that she described the annihilation of her own species in order that all others could live. While Morgan certainly understood the devastation that humans did on the face of the Earth, they also achieved wonderful things in conjunction with nature. Most people wanted a better world for their children, and the majority wanted to protect and sustain the environment. Morgan believed that the world tipped to the side of good at least 51% of the time — and that would be enough to solve the problems of the world.

Of course, ARKANE played only a tiny part in the daily fight to keep the world in balance, and she and Jake had met some truly evil people during their missions, but it had never dented her belief that humanity was fundamentally good.

Aurelia had a darker view of the world, and as Morgan glimpsed the fanatical side of the heiress, she wondered what might truly lie in Eden. Was the Garden a paradise for humans or a haven for nature without the polluters and destroyers that threatened the Earth?

"How often do we even see plants?" Aurelia continued. "We live by their grace, and yet we wander the Earth with only an occasional glance in their direction. This world should be green and yet, we turn more of it grey every day with our endless urge to expand. Why should we endlessly procreate and expand our species at the expense of all others?" She clenched her fists. "Enough. It is time for a change."

* * *

Jake tuned out Aurelia's tirade as he concentrated on Frik, his gaze fixed on the massive South African. Neither man looked away, both of them communicating wordless aggression. There was hate in Frik's eyes, but more than that, anticipation. Jake was certain that this encounter would not end in a friendly truce where they all joined in harmony to search for Eden. The only question was how it would play out.

He couldn't help but look at the scars around Frik's neck. Where once he might have felt a twinge of guilt at the part he played in the injuries, now he could only see the mutilation of Ines and imagine her death at the hands of this monster. Aurelia ranted of nature and its place in the world, while she allowed this abomination to roam free, torturing and killing.

With each slow breath, Jake focused on Frik, waiting for the move that would inevitably come. There was too much unfinished business between them.

A second later, Frik's face reddened, his eyes blazing with the anger he could no longer restrain. He took a step forward, his right hand moving to the small of his back.

As he pulled out his gun, Jake took two huge strides away from Morgan, diving and commando rolling behind the side of the statue's plinth. He trusted that she would manage Aurelia while Frik couldn't help but seek revenge on his old foe.

Gunshots pinged against the stone.

Frik was coming for him fast.

Jake grinned, the manic smile of a warrior going into battle, relishing the adrenalin of action. Bring it on.

He looked around for options. A maintenance door stood ajar just a few feet away in the statue's base with a sign permitting no entry to the public. Jake jumped up and ran, making it inside as another bullet pinged against the metal.

*   *   *

Morgan dived for the ground in the opposite direction to Jake as the first gunshot pinged on the concrete plinth.

Aurelia collapsed to the pavement beside her, curling up into a fetal position. Her bravado disappeared in the wake of actual violence, while her bodyguard left her behind to pursue his long-held revenge.

As Frik chased Jake, Morgan rolled to her feet and stood over the cowering heiress, yanking her up easily. The woman was so frail that Morgan was a little worried she would break, but under the skin, she could feel wiry muscles. The heiress was clearly tougher than she looked.

"Where are the other fragments?" Morgan demanded, trying to focus on the ultimate goal while she worried for Jake. If she went to help him, Aurelia would escape and she couldn't let that happen. Her partner was on his own.

* * *

Jake slammed the door shut behind him and rammed the lock home. It wouldn't stop Frik for long. He ran up inside the statue, taking two narrow steps at a time, rounding a corner and startling a maintenance worker.

The man put his hands up as if in surrender as Jake approached. "Por favor não me machuque."

Jake understood his gesture and nodded. "It's OK, I'm not going to hurt you. But you need to hide."

He indicated a storage cupboard. "Stay in there. Wait until it's quiet again." He put a finger to his lips.

The man understood his intention and shuffled over to the storage unit. He folded himself inside, eyes wide with fear as he pulled the door closed.

The sound of metal rattling. A gunshot. The squeak of the door opening below.

Footsteps up the staircase. Frik was inside.

Jake ran up another level. The chamber opened out just under the shoulders of Christ, with a series of maintenance ladders leading up to trapdoors overhead, each emerging on a different part of the statue.

He spun around, looking for anything that could help. The walls were plain concrete with fixed points to attach safety harnesses. But there was nothing he could use, and Frik had a gun. This tiny chamber would be a death trap against such a weapon.

Jake looked up. There was only one option. He took a deep breath and climbed one ladder, quickly pushing open the trapdoor, even as the footsteps below grew closer.

As he emerged onto the right shoulder of Christ, Jake gasped at the panoramic view before him — and the realization that nothing but air separated him from the drop below.

He scrambled onto the shoulder, lying flat, his hands clutching the thin conductive cable that bisected the statue to channel lightning strikes.

The trapdoor slammed shut behind him. Jake had one chance to disarm Frik or the fight would be over before it even started.

A creak of metal.

Frik burst up through the trapdoor, throwing off its weight with one powerful thrust. The huge bodyguard emerged out of the darkness, gun in one hand.

But Jake had the upper ground.

He kicked at Frik's face, the powerful heel strike connecting with the man's nose, breaking it. Frik roared with rage, blood streaming from the wound as he clutched at the side of the trapdoor.

Jake kicked again, this time with a scraping movement. The gun spun out of Frik's loosened grip and plummeted off the edge of the statue.

But the massive South African didn't stop. He clenched his meaty fists into hammers of flesh and pulled himself out of the trapdoor.

Jake crawled out of reach, acutely aware of the precipitous drop below. Frik stood up on the narrow shoulder. He shook his head and snorted to clear his nose, drops of blood splattering over the concrete.

"It's time you paid for what you did." He stretched out his arms for balance and took a step forward.

Jake scrambled to his feet, his senses alert as Frik edged toward him. The shoulder of Christ ended close behind, and a dizzying drop lay on either side. It was a strange place indeed for such a fight, but a sense of calm rose within Jake as he faced the man determined to kill him. He thought of the young *capoeiristas* in the plaza of Recife, the way they flowed and moved with such grace, seemingly resistant to gravity. If only he'd learned such skill.

But he was not done yet.

Frik advanced another half step and threw a punch.

Jake ducked back out of reach, but as he moved, he wobbled a little. A cold flush flooded his system as he glimpsed the ground far below. He knew that Frik would not leave the statue without killing him.

Jake clenched his fists. If he went down, he'd take the bastard with him.

CHAPTER 17

A SUDDEN CRY FROM ABOVE.

Morgan looked up as a figure tumbled from the shoulder of Christ, a dark shape silhouetted against the sun, his features obscured.

"Jake!" Morgan couldn't help his name escaping her lips.

Her heart beat faster as the body hit the concrete below the statue with a sickening thud.

Aurelia stopped struggling in her arms and they stood for a moment, both of them waiting in a beat of silence for the truth to unfold.

Another man looked over the edge of the shoulder of Christ and waved down.

It was Jake. Morgan sighed with relief and as Aurelia sagged in her arms, defeated, she couldn't help but smile. Jake had as many lives as the jungle cat he sometimes reminded her of with his muscular grace and dark amber-flecked eyes.

She dragged Aurelia up the concrete deck toward where Frik had landed.

"I don't want to see him," the heiress pleaded. "Please, just let me go."

But something in her tone was off. Morgan didn't trust the weak woman, little girl lost routine. It might work with all those alpha males she surrounded herself with, but there was a core of steel to Aurelia dos Santos Fidalgo. Morgan dragged Aurelia on.

Jake beat them to the concrete platform. He stood over

Frik's body, his face betraying a mix of emotion. Morgan knew him well enough to know it was not the killing of a man that concerned him, but the events that led to the demise of someone he had been partially responsible for creating. If Jake had not sent Frik down the mine that day, would he now be lying dead so far from his homeland?

But as with the history of the very land they stood upon, there would always be questions of how the past intersected with the present. Without the Portuguese Empire landing here five hundred years ago, would this city be what it was today? Would Christ even be the Redeemer here, or would a god of the indigenous tribes spread his arms wide to welcome travelers?

Aurelia tore herself from Morgan's grip and sank to her knees by Frik's body. She bent over the big man and laid her head on his chest as she wept. Her tears seeped into the pool of blood that spread out from his skull, dashed on the stones beneath. Had Frik been more than just a bodyguard, or was Aurelia playing for time while she figured out her next move? Morgan found the heiress hard to read as she and Jake stood in silence.

After a few minutes, Aurelia fell quiet. She turned and looked up at Jake, her dark eyes flashing with anger. "You will never find Eden. I'll never give you the other pieces. You can send me to my grave before I share their location with you."

"We will find the Garden." Jake's voice was low and menacing, certainty clear in his tone. "And we'll witness what you will never see. You'll go to your grave never knowing what could have been."

Aurelia wrung her hands together, her knuckles white as she tightened her grip along with her resolve. But Morgan saw something in her eyes, a flare of desire for the mythical place that went far beyond her need for revenge. Frik had been a love of some kind, but he was nothing to Aurelia's true passion and she was clearly weighing her options.

They had to get to Eden as fast as possible — the professor's life was at stake and the clock ticked away the seconds since she had been taken. If there was a chance they could get the pieces, they needed to take it. Morgan took a calculated risk. "What if we take you with us to Eden?"

Jake spun around in surprise, but she ignored him. They had been partners long enough that he would go with her intuition on this.

The heiress frowned. "How can I trust you?"

Morgan reached out a hand. "I can only give you my word."

"And mine," Jake said after a moment. "If you give us the other pieces of the map, we'll find Eden together. When we reach the Garden, this agreement is over and you're on your own. But until then, we can put aside our differences and work together."

Something like triumph flashed in Aurelia's eyes, and she gave a half-smile. She took Morgan's hand, shaking it as she rose to her feet, the body behind her forgotten.

"That is enough for now. I'll take you to the other pieces of the map. They're not far away."

* * *

Once they were airborne again, Aurelia directed the pilot to head downtown, flying over the city to the north-east. They landed on the rooftop of a modern skyscraper, the Fidalgo headquarters.

As the rotors spun gently to a stop, Aurelia looked out the window with a wistful gaze. "I'm just a figurehead here now. My search for Eden is the very opposite of what the company would want. They have no wish to see me here, but it's close to where the pieces are and the easiest place to land. We'll go straight down in the elevator and out onto the street."

They clambered out of the helicopter and headed into the building.

True to her word, Aurelia did not even stop to greet anyone. In fact, it seemed as if people who might have boarded the elevator saw her and chose to take another route. Others scurried away at her approach. Morgan noticed how Aurelia's spine stiffened and how she wrung her thin hands as they descended. For all her wealth, it seemed the heiress truly was a pariah in the empire her father had built.

They exited the office building and emerged onto the busy streets of the Centro district, the historic and financial hub of the city. Morgan and Jake kept close to Aurelia as they hurried through the warren of streets.

Eventually, they emerged into a wide open square with the hand-cut Portuguese paving stones reminiscent of Lisbon and Macau, but this was no thriving plaza where tourists could sit and drink coffee in the sun.

There were a few sparse trees for a splash of green, and a geometric modern sculpture with faded yellow paint, but the buildings surrounding the square were rundown and covered with graffiti. While Morgan appreciated urban street art when it had an element of beauty or a message to consider, this was just ugly tagging and spray-painted scrawl. It didn't seem like a place Aurelia would frequent.

But as they walked across the square, Morgan caught sight of their true destination. The Real Gabinete Português de Leitura, the Royal Portuguese Cabinet of Reading, stood like a proud sentinel at the opposite end of the square, the repository of the largest collection of Portuguese works outside of Portugal. Built in a Gothic-Renaissance style, its high arched windows were marked with ornate crosses and the delicate stone filigree brought to mind the Jeronimos Monastery in Belém back in Lisbon. Four statues looked out onto the square; Pedro Álvares Cabral, the discoverer of Brazil, Vasco da Gama, the first European to reach India, and Morgan also recognized Henry the Navigator, who inspired the Age of Discovery.

She pointed to the fourth statue. "Who's that?"

Aurelia looked up with a smile. "Luís de Camões, Portugal's greatest poet whose work is considered in the same realm as Shakespeare, Homer or Dante. 'Time changes, and our desires change. What we believe — even what we are — is ever changing.'" She shrugged. "So says the poet, but can we ever really change?"

They entered the library, and Aurelia nodded at the guard by the entrance. He waved them through, clearly accustomed to her visits. They walked through the corridors toward the Reading Room.

"*Time* magazine named this as the fourth most beautiful library in the world," Aurelia said. "It has been my sanctuary. Whenever I was forced to attend the company headquarters and endure days of meetings and legal matters, I would schedule time to come here and sit in the silence and read. This is where I first found mention of the map to Eden, so it is only right that we end it here. Come, I stored the pieces with my research."

Aurelia pushed open the door to the Reading Room and Morgan looked around in wonder, Jake motionless by her side as they both took in its grandeur.

Three stories of bookshelves encased in dark wood flanked the room with spiral pillars highlighted in gold around them, while geometric shapes etched in black stone bisected the white and grey marble flagstones beneath. Above the shelves, beyond the reach of even the tallest library ladders, a golden canopy stretched up to a stained glass window bringing light into this haven of learning. Sixteen individual antique desks provided places for scholars to work, but only two were occupied, and those working studiously ignored the newcomers.

Aurelia walked softly into the library and led Morgan

and Jake up a staircase to the second level, the old wood creaking underfoot.

Morgan appreciated the almost religious atmosphere of the library. She felt closer to whatever might be called God in a house of learning than she did in a traditional place of worship. She wanted to run her fingers over the spines of these old books and dislodge the dust of antiquity. She didn't speak Portuguese, but Morgan thought that some books might communicate their meaning through mere physical proximity. At least, that's what she told herself when her book pile back home in Jericho, Oxford, teetered on the edge of overflowing. Owning books meant possessing the knowledge within, and that was sometimes as good as reading it. If that was true, this place was rich indeed.

Aurelia stopped at one particular bookcase and pulled down an oversized tome, a historical book of botanical illustrations with intricate labeling. She opened it to reveal a plastic folder and inside, the two pieces of the manuscript from Amsterdam and Macau.

Jake reached over and took them out of the book, his gaze fixed on Aurelia. Anger flared in her eyes for a moment, and then she nodded her agreement.

Morgan exhaled a breath she didn't even know she'd been holding. They finally had all the pieces of the map. They were going to find Eden.

CHAPTER 18

WHEN MARTIN KLEIN STEPPED off the plane, Morgan couldn't help but give a fond smile. His shock of blonde hair spiked up all over the place, his jacket was done up with the wrong buttons and he jerked away from people around him to maintain his need for personal space. He carried a small backpack with everything he needed for this short trip to help them with the mission. Most would consider him unusual, many might even use the word 'special' in a way that wasn't a compliment. But few understood how special Martin really was, and Morgan was grateful that she was one of them.

They had grown close over the missions they had experienced together with Jake. Although Martin wasn't a natural field agent, his knowledge and ability to think differently had often proved to be the missing link that the team needed to discover the next step. His rational and unemotional approach had helped in the past, but this time, Morgan knew the journey was personal. Martin had shaken off the effects of the poison but Sebastian was still in hospital, Professor Camara Mbaye remained missing, and he blamed himself for involving them.

Martin looked up and Morgan lifted a hand to wave a greeting as he hurried over.

"You have all the pieces?" he asked, his eagerness hard to contain. He bounced up and down on the balls of his feet with no need to rest after the long flight from London to Rio de Janeiro.

Morgan nodded as she led him toward the taxi rank. "Yes, we've got an office suite at the Fidalgo mining headquarters reserved for our investigation." She shrugged as they jumped in a cab. "Strange times make for strange bedfellows, indeed. I'm glad you're here to help."

During the journey into the city, Martin tapped his long fingers on his knees, as if limbering up for the code he would soon generate, and the taxi soon pulled up outside the towering skyscraper.

Morgan flashed her temporary identification, and the guard let them through and into the bank of shining chrome elevators. They sped up to the penthouse suite that Aurelia had commandeered for their preparation to travel east, leveraging her remaining authority to get them the resources they needed.

Jake stood with the heiress in a glass-fronted meeting room before an oversized whiteboard covered in scrawled handwriting. He waved as they passed, indicating that he would be out soon. Aurelia glanced over with barely concealed disdain. The woman clearly had a penchant for strong South African men, and Morgan was happy for Jake to take the lead in managing her — at least for now.

She led Martin into a smaller room kept with blinds closed down over the full-length glass walls and overhead lights dimmed low enough to protect the pieces of ancient manuscript laid out on the table. There was an extensive amount of other equipment in the room, everything they might need to investigate the map further.

Martin whistled a little under his breath. "Finally together again."

Morgan nodded. "It's likely that they haven't been this way since 1496, when the Jews were expelled from Portugal and scattered across the empire." As she said the words, a sense of foreboding rose within. Whoever made this map went to a lot of trouble to make sure the pieces were separated when it was a lifetime's journey to travel across the globe.

But why not destroy the map altogether?

She tried to imagine the person who created it. Perhaps some old Rabbi, desperate to save the rare knowledge but afraid for its future potential. Did he rip it apart with tears in his eyes at the thought of what might be lost? There was no way to know how it had come into being, or what the map might lead to in reality. Perhaps there was nothing there at all. But at least now they could find out.

Martin opened his backpack and pulled out a slim laptop through which he could access the ARKANE servers. But first, they needed to know what to search for, and that's where Morgan appreciated Martin's different way of looking at things.

The map was now complete — but it was not a simple, modern geographical layout with a clear path. A verdant garden lay at the center of four rivers with phrases written around its heart, interwoven with faded images of many kinds of trees, plants and flowers.

But there was something wrong about it. Morgan didn't know what it could be, but the map looked unfinished in some inexplicable way.

Martin stared down at the fragments, his brow furrowed in concentration, clearly feeling the same way. They had both seen enough ancient maps and manuscripts in their time and researched a lot more. Both found this one unusual.

"There must be something more…" Martin whispered.

A moment later, he brightened. "Of course! Bring it over here."

He turned on a light box with a glass top, back-lit with bulbs that enabled different layers to be seen within whatever lay above. "Many of the Kabbalist manuscripts in particular use different kinds of ink visible in certain lights. This should give us a new perspective."

Morgan carefully placed the pieces on top and as light flooded through, the pigments deepened in color. Greens split into shades of dark moss and emerald, and the bark of the tree shifted into shiny chestnut with walnut hues. The vines seemed to shimmer as spines of silver emerged with razor-sharp, wicked blades. More text appeared, the writing almost frenzied, and there were droplets of something darker on the page. Rust perhaps... or blood.

This wasn't a map to a gentle Eden. This was a warning to stay away.

"Can you decipher the text?" Morgan said, bending closer. "It looks a bit like Hebrew, but not something I can understand."

"Let's see what we can do." Martin picked up a handheld scanner and ran it over the map, holding it just an inch or so above. Once the scan was complete, a digital image appeared on his computer screen.

He sat down and typed so rapidly that Morgan could barely see his fingers as they flashed over the keys. It was a pleasure to watch Martin at work, and she felt privileged that he allowed her to see him like this.

The world fell away as he worked with the tools he had developed for ARKANE, delving into databases linked by strange coincidences using ancient keywords in dead languages. He accessed the machine learning algorithms he had trained to discover new information, hidden to even the most knowledgeable human brain.

Occasionally, Martin stopped and pushed his glasses up or ran his fingers through his shock of blonde hair, pulling it into spikes. He narrowed his eyes and stared at the lines of code on the screen, some programmed by his own hand, still more generated by the extension of his genius, the computer itself.

While Morgan was confident of her place in the physical world, sure of her ability to find the objects they sought, her brain could only fathom so much, while Martin's world stretched into places far beyond human knowing.

She thought of her father, a Kabbalist scholar, murdered as one of the Remnant and avenged at the Gates of Hell. Leon Sierra had worn this same concentrated expression as he studied the words of the Torah, as the letters spun themselves into meaning that gave him an insight into his impenetrable God. Did Martin feel the same way as understanding clicked into place and new perceptions surfaced? Perhaps one day she would ask him, but for now, Morgan sat in silence as her friend conducted a symphony of code.

The clicking of keys marked the passing of time until Martin finally stopped. His screen changed to show a map of the Middle East with the dominant lines of the rivers Tigris and Euphrates, and next to it, the scan of the fragments with the translated text.

He removed his glasses and rubbed his eyes. "The hidden text was the key to understanding where the rivers intersect." He zoomed into the map. "A document chronicling the Islamic invasion of the Caucasus in the eighth century mentions a River Gaihun, later renamed Araxes and then Aras. Some early Victorian biblical commentaries have it as Gihon-Aras."

Martin pointed to the screen. "It rises in the mountains to the north of Lake Van in south-eastern Turkey and runs to the Caspian Sea across northern Iran."

"So where is the Pishon?" Morgan asked.

He zoomed the display closer. "The database pulled from various linguistic models and determined that the Hebrew was likely conflated with ancient Iranian. The Pishon is actually the Qizil Üzan, a tributary which also runs into the Caspian Sea."

Martin superimposed the proposed rivers over the map, and Morgan took a step back in surprise. The four lines clearly outlined a region that crossed from eastern Turkey through Armenia and Azerbaijan, circling down through northern Iran.

"So if that region is Eden, then where's the Garden?"

Martin zoomed in to Lake Urmia and followed a line of blue east through Tabriz, the fourth largest city in Iran, in the north-western corner of the country near the borders of Turkey, Armenia, and Azerbaijan. "This is the Ari Chay River, once known as the Meidan, Persian for walled garden."

Morgan nodded. "OK, but that's still a vast area."

Martin zoomed in once more to the peak of Sahand Mountain, a dormant volcano to the south of Tabriz.

"Ezekiel, chapter 28. 'You were in Eden, the garden of God... You were on the holy mount of God; you walked among the fiery stones.'"

"Fiery stones," repeated Morgan in wonder. "It could be the place. God is often found on a mountain-top."

"It's known as the bride of Iran's mountains because of its abundant and beautiful landscape." Martin pointed to the eastern slopes. "There's a ski resort on one flank, but there's a Protected Area on the opposite side. There are no maps I can find of it, which is unusual, even for that part of the world, and Professor Mbaye had a dig site in the area before it was abruptly shut down."

Morgan gazed at the contours of the mountain. "Then that's where we'll go next."

CHAPTER 19

Tabriz, Iran

The taxi sped past the industrial outskirts of the city, and as dusk fell, Morgan thought about the last time she and Jake were in Tabriz together. They had found the Pentecost stone of Thaddeus the Apostle in the church of St Mary, considered by some to be the second oldest church in the world after Bethlehem in Israel.

Although their mission was successful, they had not left the chapel quietly. ARKANE cleaned up after their agents and smoothed a path with diplomatic relationships maintained over centuries, but it was possible that her face and Jake's were on some Iranian hit list. Given her Israeli heritage, Morgan did not want to end up in prison here. The possibility made her more nervous than usual, but their passports were clean and they were officially here to hike Kamal Daghi, the highest peak of Sahand Mountain. Aurelia had arranged exploration permits through her business contacts, and there was no real reason for concern, but Morgan couldn't shake the foreboding that twisted her guts. She gazed out the window, trying to distract herself.

This area of Iran was an archaeological paradise, but few could visit due to centuries of invasion, war and neglect. Tabriz was a mix of architecture from millennia ago to skyscrapers of the industrial age: the fifteenth-century Blue

Mosque with its exquisite decorative tiles; the historic souk with its vaulted brick archways; and even the Mausoleum of Poets with a thousand years of venerated writers entombed within. But all these things lay behind them as they drove south-east from the city.

Jake leaned in close enough that Morgan could smell the pine forest of his aftershave. "You're quiet," he said.

"Just thinking about what might be ahead."

Aurelia looked up from her phone at their words, scowling a little as she tried to get a signal. They were an unexpected trio and Morgan still didn't trust the heiress, but she also knew that the woman was deeply committed to finding Eden. Until they saw the Garden or its walls, they had the same mission. Then all bets were off.

It started to rain by the time they left the highway and headed into the mountainous Sahand Protected Area. As the car wove its way up the steep side of a gorge, a dense mist descended, shrouding the cliffs in grey shadow. The driver seemed oblivious to the precipitous drop as he swerved around a sharp corner. Morgan clutched the door handle with white knuckles and was perversely satisfied to see Aurelia do the same, her face almost green with nausea as they rose higher into the forbidding landscape.

Just as Morgan was about ready to throw up, the taxi rounded a final corner and the mist cleared a little to reveal the unusual landscape of Kandovan village. It lay in the foothills of Sahand Mountain and looked more like a collection of giant termite mounds than a dwelling place for humans. The villagers had lived within these structures made from volcanic material for generations, with some estimates of the area being inhabited over six thousand years ago. The locals had expanded their houses by carving out new caves and adding stone and brick to link the little town together.

"I hope our guide is here already," Aurelia muttered, as they emerged from the taxi into freezing rain and a cold wind. "I am not going to wait around in this."

The tone of entitlement in her voice made Morgan smile, but she agreed with the sentiment.

The three of them grabbed their packs from the back of the car and turned to face the village. Handmade wooden doors remained shut to keep out the rain, and Morgan felt like a true outsider in this faraway place. If Aurelia's contact did not come through, the trip would be over before it even started.

A light flickered from further up a stone staircase that wound between two of the structures.

"Come up, come up. Be welcome!" The sound of foot-steps came from the stairwell, and a young Iranian man emerged from the shadows. He had the close-cropped dark hair and neat beard of many locals, but with light blue eyes that indicated a mixed ancestry from the north. "I'm Darius, your guide. Come inside and rest by the fire."

Darius insisted on transporting Morgan and Aurelia's packs, while Jake carried his own up the stairs. They reached a tiny wooden entrance to one of the volcanic houses and went inside, closing the door against the rising storm.

It was warm and cozy within the naturally insulated structure, made even more welcoming by woven rugs that lay on the floor and hung on the walls. Three low couches heaped with cushions and blankets sat around a central wooden table laden with a generous platter of Sangak flat-bread and local honey alongside dried apricots and figs. The smell of mint tea hung in the air from a steaming samovar.

Now they were further from the city, Morgan was able to relax and the sweet taste of honey with figs helped bring her into the present moment. The dark sense of foreboding still lingered, but she pushed it away as they ate.

Darius explained how they would summit the mountain. "We leave two hours before dawn. I'll guide you up the old paths my family has walked for generations. The weather is due to clear, but we'll probably walk in the rain for a while."

He waved his hand as if swatting away a fly. "No matter. The views will be worth it from the top and I'll show you where you can camp while you do your sampling."

Morgan nodded in agreement. Their cover story was a survey of ancient volcanos in the region, and they were here to take rock samples — at least that's what Darius had been told. He would come up after two days and help them back down the mountain again, but hopefully, they wouldn't need that long to find their goal.

"The Sahand Protected Area is a rich ecological domain," Darius explained. "You need to watch out for some animals, like wild cats and brown bears, but it's more likely that you'll only see some Armenian mouflon." He made spirals in the air with his fingers. "Rams with huge curved horns."

Morgan recalled the biblical story of Abraham taking his son Isaac to the summit of Mount Moriah. On the verge of sacrificing his only child as a burnt offering, God sent an angel to stay his hand and a ram to offer in place of his son. There were so many echoes of Genesis here, and despite the warmth of the room, Morgan shivered. The first book of the Bible was a tale of murder, betrayal, destruction and ecological catastrophe. She could only hope that their fate would be better in the coming days.

After they had eaten, Darius turned down the lamps and indicated the couches. "Rest here. I'll knock when it's time to set out."

Aurelia curled up and tugged several blankets over her thin form. The covering dwarfed her, and Morgan wondered how a woman with such oversized drive and passion could be sustained by so little physical presence. The heiress both fascinated and repelled her at the same time. There was so much she could not understand about the woman, but pondering it would have to wait. She lay down on her back and tried to clear her mind.

Jake rested against the cushions, his head close to hers. "What do you think we'll find tomorrow?"

Morgan shrugged. "I really don't know. It could be point-less, but we've seen so many unexpected things together. Anything is possible."

Jake sighed. "You make anything possible."

He spoke so softly that Morgan didn't know whether she really heard the words at all.

* * *

A sharp rap on the door woke Morgan from strange dreams woven from mist and shadow. Jake was already up and opened the door to let Darius in.

The sound of a donkey braying came from outside. It wasn't luxury travel, but it was the best they would get in this area and suited their academic cover.

The smell of freshly brewed coffee helped encourage Morgan out of her nest of cushions. Darius set a flask on the table and gathered some small glasses.

"Here, drink this quickly and then we'll get going."

Morgan took her shot of thick, strong coffee like medi-cine. Jake followed suit with a shake of his head at the bitter aftertaste. Aurelia couldn't help the revulsion on her face as she tasted it, but she drank it down anyway, all of them needing the extra caffeine after only a few hours of sleep.

The sound of rain hammered on the stone outside, but there was no time to wait for finer weather. They pulled on waterproof gear and head-torches and stepped out into the darkness.

Darius slung tents and provisions into panniers either side of a donkey held steady by a teenage boy. "My nephew," he explained. "He'll follow behind. Now, we climb."

Darius led the small group up a winding rocky path away from the village, the ground slippery from the rain. They walked in silence and Morgan relaxed into the strenuous ascent, her breathing settling into a rhythm as she found her stride. Nowhere else to be but here, nothing else to do but walk. There was a kind of meditation in that.

The sky lightened as the hours passed and the rain grew softer until it was just a fine drizzle. The terrain emerged from the gloom, scrubland and rocky slopes with a smattering of snow higher up, with deep ravines either side of the path. Morgan noticed some shy purple wildflowers peeking out from under the scree, a tasty morsel for the mountain goats endemic to the area.

Darius finally stopped in the shelter of three enormous boulders, thrust out of the volcano at some point in history and now forming a natural protection against the unpredictable weather.

"We'll set up your camp here, and you can go in any of these directions to take your samples." He put his hands out to either side and brought them together to show the arc of exploration.

"But do not go behind the volcano. That is restricted." He frowned and shook his head. "Some say it's mined and patrolled by the military. Others say it's cursed. We don't know what is true, but several villagers have disappeared with no trace of them found. So please, do not go there."

Darius and his nephew unpacked the panniers while Jake and Aurelia set up camp.

Morgan stood silently, her face turned toward the dormant volcano. Could Eden really lie beyond those slopes? There was only one way to find out.

* * *

Deep under the volcano, the Abbot turned as a young Brother ran into the sanctuary, his breath ragged from the swift journey, his eyes wide with panic.

160

"What is it, my son?"

"A new camp." The Brother panted as he struggled to catch his breath. "They've set up tents on the eastern side within walking distance of the entrance. They came with a man from the village."

"How many?"

The Brother shrugged a little. "Perhaps three who will remain when the villager and his boy leave." He stood tall and clenched his fists. "Shall I take some of the others over there tonight? Their camp is near a ravine. It wouldn't take much."

The Abbot turned to look at the woman bound with spiked vines to a wooden chair in front of the great carved door. Blood dripped from tiny wounds caused by the sharp thorns and her head hung on her chest, defeated by his interrogation. There was nothing left to learn from the professor, and the Garden needed a sacrifice. But perhaps he could give Her more than just one body to devour this time.

He spoke softly. "Let them come."

CHAPTER 20

AFTER DARIUS AND HIS nephew headed back down the mountain, Morgan helped Jake finish setting up camp. They pitched three separate tents and organized gear for an exploratory hike. Aurelia sat on a rock, watching them work, her face pale, her thin frame weak from the morning's exertion.

"Is she going to make it any further?" Jake said under his breath as they packed up some climbing gear.

Morgan glanced over at the heiress. Beneath her fragile exterior, Aurelia had a steel resolve that could overcome any physical weakness if the goal was in sight. But were they really close to the Garden? It was hard to tell what was myth and what was reality. Perhaps this was merely a place that had taken on an ancient name for a purpose lost in time.

It didn't matter at this point. Morgan was determined to find Eden. Not for any reason of faith, but to find the professor and bring her home. After the tragic end of their last mission on the island of Alcatraz, and the undeserving death of Ines, Morgan could not leave anyone behind and she knew that Jake felt the same way. Aurelia had her reasons to be here, and the Garden — or lack of it — would determine her next steps, but Morgan had no doubt the heiress would make it to the end.

"She'll be fine. Let's go find Paradise."

They assembled appropriate backpacks with scientific equipment and permits proving their reason for being on the mountain. It was doubtful that the Iranian government had a base out here, but they had to be ready just in case. If caught trespassing, they would pretend to be bumbling academics who had lost their way and hopefully, ARKANE's contacts and Aurelia's wealth would get them out. Whatever the possibilities, they had to take the risk.

Martin Klein had identified an area of the volcano's far slope inside the Protected Zone that looked like a possible area to explore. Multi-spectral satellite imaging used for archaeological research indicated a series of chambers underground and ancient tunnels hollowed out under the mountain, buried over time by the shifting of tectonic plates.

After adjusting her pack so it sat comfortably on her frame, Morgan held a map out in front of her and orientated the area against visible landmarks. The terrain was similar to areas she had hiked with packs far heavier than this during her time with the Israel Defense Force, and she had navigated under fire many times, but something about this place made her uneasy.

She found a route on the map and pointed to a faint path that headed around the southern slope of the volcano along the ridge of the ravine. "We'll go that way. The path looks like it winds around and down."

Jake hefted on his pack and helped Aurelia with her much smaller one, and they set off along the track with Morgan leading the way. She tried to modulate her natural walking pace so that the heiress could keep up. It was clear that she and Jake would make much faster progress without her, but they had made a deal, and Morgan intended to see it through.

Aurelia's clarity of purpose fascinated her, a genuine faith that the Garden held an answer to the Earth's renewal. Morgan's own faith had never been so certain. It oscillated between skepticism on the one hand, a desire to show that history, science and archaeology could explain that which others called faith. On the other hand, she specialized in the psychology of religion and researched why people did things in the name of God. She had joined ARKANE to help find answers to the questions that lay deep inside as well as for academic curiosity — and the addictive adrenalin of their missions. Morgan had witnessed the faith of so many, including her father's unwavering trust in Kabbalah wisdom, but she had never found her own enduring belief. Would she find it here at the fabled Garden, or would she be cast out once more in an echo of the Fall?

They walked for several hours without seeing much change in the landscape, circling the side of the volcano with careful steps on the rocky ground. A few mountain goats kept them company, springing along a series of boulders higher up, but Morgan had a sense that someone else watched them too, and tracked their progress over the mountain.

When they stopped to rest, Aurelia sat on the ground and sipped at her water bottle while she recovered her breath.

Jake led Morgan out of earshot. "Someone's following us, I'm sure of it."

She nodded. "More than one, perhaps. But if this is such a protected area, why haven't they shown themselves? Why haven't they warned us away? There aren't even any signs."

Jake stared out across the rocky terrain, scanning for movement in the rocks. "Darius said that villagers disappeared up here without a trace. Perhaps whoever it is wants us to proceed?"

"Then let's give them what they want." Morgan looked down at the map. "It's not much further."

They walked on and finally rounded the edge of the volcano, emerging onto a high plateau carpeted with wildflowers of every color and shape, an abundance of natural beauty.

"We must be close," Aurelia said, her expression alive with wonder as she bent to touch one flower with a gentle fingertip. "The Garden cannot be contained, and She rules here, I can feel it."

Despite the surrounding beauty, Morgan sensed eyes upon them once more. This felt less like a garden and more like a honey trap, leading them with sweetness into ruin.

Jake pointed ahead. "There's something unusual about those boulders. They don't look like a natural formation."

They walked across the meadow, Aurelia picking her way slowly as she tried to avoid stepping on the blooms. An impossible task as they lay so thickly upon the ground. She soon gave up, almost running to catch Morgan and Jake as they strode to the rock formation beyond.

The seven enormous boulders were similar to the ones they camped beside, rocks expelled from the volcano in its active years, but these were placed in a protective circular arrangement. Morgan weaved her way between them into the center, following Jake's path. They emerged on the edge of a fissure, a stony descent into the heart of the mountain. Thick green moss coated the rocks around the entrance with more wildflowers entangled within.

Morgan knelt on the side and shone her flashlight into the darkness. The edges of the cave beneath were rough and well-textured. They could definitely get down there with climbing ropes.

The sound of dripping water came from below, and it smelled of minerals with a tang of metal. Could this possibly be the entrance to Eden? It seemed at odds with the myth of an abundant garden, but if there had ever truly been such a place, it would be thousands of years old now. Perhaps buried by time, or volcanic eruption.

Morgan looked over to Jake. "What do you think?"

He shrugged. "This is the right area, and we don't have any other options. Let's at least go down and investigate further."

Aurelia stood with her back against one boulder, staring

at the hole with trepidation. She wrung her hands together as she whispered, "This is not how it's meant to be."

Morgan spun around, her frustration with the heiress spilling over. "How do you even know what it's meant to be? The idea of a mythical garden spans across many religions. You don't have a monopoly on Eden."

Jake put a hand on her arm. "None of us know what might lie ahead, so let's go have a look." He pulled ropes and carabiners out of his backpack. "Let me get this set up and we can descend together."

Once he had installed the equipment safely, Jake descended into the fissure. A few minutes later, he called up. "You definitely need to see this."

Morgan helped Aurelia down and then followed the descent, careful to keep her footing on the slippery rocks. The last thing they needed was an injury out of reach of even ARKANE's emergency help.

She touched down on the floor of the rocky cave and removed the harness, feeling the chill of cold air on her skin as weak sunlight faded overhead. As she turned around, Morgan caught her breath at the magnificent sight.

Two gigantic creatures stood either side of a narrow channel through the rock, carved from the volcano itself, with the powerful body of a bull, the head of a man and the wings of an eagle. Every intricate spiral on their beards, every feather on their wings, and every muscle was etched in fine detail, and they gazed straight ahead, eyes fixed on potential prey who dared to tread the stone of this hallowed place. For such ancient sculptures, they were in excellent condition, protected from the elements down here in the cave system.

Aurelia walked up to one and reached out a thin arm to touch the rock. She stopped mere inches away, as if she couldn't bear to know whether this place was truly real.

"They're *lamassu*," Morgan said, her voice echoing in

the cave. "Sumerian deities used by the Assyrians on their temples. This is similar to the Gate of Xerxes in the ruins of Persepolis."

Jake walked to the rock face and stared up at one figure. "I thought the book of Genesis said that God put cherubim on the east side of the Garden of Eden to guard the way." He frowned. "Aren't they cute fat children with wings and nothing like these?"

Morgan shook her head. "Cherubim were never cute. The book of Ezekiel describes them as whirling wheels covered with eyes, four faces and gigantic wings. These might be different from that exact description, but they are certainly scary winged creatures. Besides, why would God choose something cute to guard the way?"

"Eden is far more than a biblical myth." Aurelia spat the words, her eyes flashing with anger as she turned to face them. "It is the ancient Garden of the Earth Mother, the Goddess who ruled this planet before a masculine God was ever invented."

Her sudden anger was interesting — and dangerous. Morgan saw that Jake was about to say something and she put a hand up to stop him. There was no point in arguing with fanatics, and Aurelia would not listen to any kind of intellectual discussion at this point. Morgan had no allegiance to a particular tradition of Eden, but clearly, Aurelia had a fixed view of what lay ahead.

"Whatever it might be," Morgan said. "We can only know for sure if we continue. Together, if you like."

Aurelia took a deep breath and sagged back against the stone wall. "I'm sorry. It's just overwhelming to think that we might almost be there, after everything I've done to find it."

The heiress looked exhausted, and Morgan tried to recall when she'd last seen Aurelia eat. She seemed to subsist on air and water, but her energy was obviously starting to fail.

"If we're going to proceed, we need to go now," Jake said

softly. "We only have a few more hours of daylight and we don't have the gear to camp down here. Let's check out the next chamber quickly and then return tomorrow with more equipment."

He peered down the corridor between the giant statues and shone his torch into the darkness. "This looks pretty long and narrow. We need to go in single file." He turned to Aurelia. "You OK with this?"

She nodded. "Yes, I want to see it. Let's go on."

Jake led the way, Aurelia behind, and Morgan brought up the rear.

As she stepped between the gigantic figures, the chill in the air deepened as if cold seeped from the surrounding rocks. Her sense of foreboding grew stronger once more, and as she thought of the many eyes of the cherubim, Morgan could almost feel them watching.

They trespassed in this place, that much was clear. But who else was down here with them, and what waited in the shadows beyond?

CHAPTER 21

JAKE'S HEAD-TORCH ILLUMINATED the way through the narrow tunnel, but the dark stone around absorbed much of the light, dampening it to a mere flicker. There were rough markings on the rock where ancient tools wielded by muscled hands had once chipped away at the heart of the volcano. It reminded him of the men who had descended into the mine back in South Africa, and his own part in creating the man that Frik eventually became. Jake recalled the South African's face at the moment he toppled from the shoulder of Christ, knocked off balance by his own ferocious charge. He still raged at his enemy even as he plummeted to the concrete below. Jake had seen death in many guises, but something about the big South African haunted him.

He pushed away the dark thoughts. Now was not the time to dwell on past mistakes. He could only focus on making sure this mission succeeded, and right now, that was not certain at all.

After ten minutes of walking, the tunnel narrowed even further and Jake had to squeeze his body through sideways. He took his pack off to drag behind him. If the passage constricted anymore, they'd have to turn back.

To be honest, he wanted to get out of here. The stone tunnel was a tight, immovable prison. The walls felt like they were closing in. The lack of airflow made his breath ragged. The temperature was rising. Jake couldn't help but think of the millions of tons of rock above him, crushing down, pressing, constricting —

He shook his head to clear the thoughts. This place was claustrophobic enough without dwelling on it. He shifted focus and considered the strategic positioning of the narrow tunnel. The end would be a choke point and each would have to emerge alone to whatever waited beyond. Turned to the side as he was, he would struggle to defend himself and that made him seriously uneasy.

"Stop!" Aurelia shouted behind him in the tunnel, her labored breathing suddenly short and fast in what sounded like a panic attack.

"I have to get out!" she screamed as she banged her thin arms against Jake's pack from behind. "Please help me…" Her voice trailed off into piteous sobs.

"Close your eyes," Morgan said in a calm voice. "You're OK. Take some deep breaths."

"We're almost there." Jake's upbeat tone hid the fact that he had no idea when the tunnel would end. But surely it couldn't go on forever.

He moved faster, ignoring the squeeze of rock against his broad shoulders as he pushed on down the tunnel. Aurelia was tiny, with more space to move, and her sobs quietened as she controlled her fear once more. But Jake knew she might collapse if they did not emerge soon. He understood how exhausting a panic attack could be. They had to get out of here.

Suddenly, he saw a light in the distance, a flicker of flame. Jake turned off his torch for a second to check it was real. The warm glow flared against the darkness ahead.

"I see the exit," he called back to Aurelia and Morgan, redoubling his pace. "Come on, we're almost there."

But as Jake drew closer to the end, he could see figures waiting for them. Monks in forest green robes positioned in a fighting stance, hoods obscuring their faces, each holding a huge sword. The Order of the Ignis Flammae.

Jake stifled a groan. Killer monks were never his favorite foe. They were fanatics, all of them keen to die for their cause and ready to meet their Maker. He had no desire to see God anytime soon, but it was too late to turn back now.

"We've got company," he called back softly, making sure that Morgan knew what was coming.

He stepped into the chamber at the end of the tunnel, dropping his pack and raising both his hands in surrender. Aurelia stumbled out behind him and dropped to her hands and knees, panting and coughing as she tried to draw breath. Morgan walked out slowly, scanning the surroundings with a calm gaze, and once again, Jake was glad to have her by his side. Whatever happened, they had each other's back.

Five monks stood around them, swords drawn and pointed at the new arrivals. Their faces were mostly obscured but Jake glimpsed some of the men beneath. They were all well-muscled, clearly highly trained, and each held his sword high with unwavering strength. These were not men he cared to fight.

The chamber was long and wide, almost an underground cathedral in its grandeur. Tall bronze candelabra stood at the sides, casting a warm glow across the stone, next to heavy wooden barrels stacked in alcoves down the cave. More light emanated from the long fire pit in the central aisle. Coals smoldered in the center, generating heat that made the place stifling hot. Jake swiftly took an inventory of the place, assessing their options. There must be a ventilation system and other ways to bring in supplies. There was no way those barrels came in through the tight tunnel they had just emerged from.

He heard a sharp intake of breath beside him.

Jake turned to see Morgan staring down the central nave to the end of the chamber where a gigantic ancient door stood, carved with botanical images. In front of it, there was a stone altar, and a figure tied on top. Professor Camara Mbaye.

Morgan took a step toward her prone figure.

The monks tightened the circle, raising their swords higher in an obvious threat.

Morgan stopped, palms open in submission as she moved back into place.

"Enough." A deep voice echoed in the chamber and the monks took a step back at the command, bringing their weapons down to hold at their sides, alert and ready.

An old man walked into the circle. "I am the Abbot of the Order of the Ignis Flammae. Few outsiders have ever made it this far, but your presence answers a question we have pondered for centuries. Back in the 1500s, one of the Brothers was a New Christian, a forced convert from Judaism. When he discovered what lay at the heart of the Garden, he saw a way to give the Jews leverage against the Inquisition. He made a map and gave it to a Rabbi in Portugal, who split it into pieces and distributed it across the empire. We've tried to find it over the years, but figured it was lost in time." He shrugged. "No matter, you're here now and you can join your friend."

He glanced over to Camara. "That one has little left to give, but what she has will soon be offered to the Garden. You're a welcome addition to the sacrifice."

Jake noticed Morgan clench her fists at his words and then relax them again as she controlled her anger. Clearly, they weren't going to be skewered immediately or thrown into the pit of coals, so they could afford to wait and see what happened next. Every moment they stayed alive, opened up another possible future.

Aurelia struggled to her feet. "I've sought the Garden my entire life." Her voice wavered a little, and she wiped a tear from her eye as if overcome by the moment. "Please, let me see it."

The Abbot smiled. "Of course, my child. You will be the first inside."

His tone was gentle, but Jake noticed the predatory look in his eyes. The Garden was no peaceful haven.

"Bring them." The Abbot spun around and walked the length of the chamber.

Morgan didn't need any encouragement. She followed the Abbot, one monk by her side, to make sure she didn't try anything.

Jake helped Aurelia while she was still a little wobbly as the monks escorted them to the altar.

*   *   *

Morgan couldn't help herself. As the Abbot walked behind the altar to stand in front of the door, she ran to Camara. The monk behind her brought up his sword, but the Abbot raised a hand to stop him as Morgan bent to the prone figure.

She had never met the professor before, but Camara was only here because ARKANE had involved her in the mission. As Morgan touched the professor's neck and checked for a pulse, she was determined that Dr Mbaye would make it out of here.

There was a faint beating under her fingertips.

She sighed with relief. Camara had been tortured, the bloody marks on her body and bruised face were testament to that, but at least she was alive.

The Abbot smiled at her efforts. "Oh, don't worry, my child. I would never have killed her. She's an offering to the Garden she has tried so hard to find. And she brought you to us, so the sacrifice will be all the greater. Lord be praised."

He stood aside, revealing the giant door in all its glory. Made from ancient wood and etched with writhing vines and blooming flowers, its petals gaped wide in voracious maws, while its leaves dripped with poison. A curious portal to what must surely be Eden, it spoke of unrelenting hunger, a desire to possess the Earth and everything in it.

The Abbot began to chant, his deep voice a sonorous

boom in the cavern as he unlocked the door with an over-sized antique key.

The monks around joined him in a chorus, their voices rising to the roof. The words were indistinguishable, some archaic language preserved by the ancient Brotherhood — but the sentiment was clear. It was more a battle chant than a hymn of praise; a declaration of war, not a song of worship.

Whatever lay behind the door must be faced with courage.

Morgan steeled herself as two of the monks dragged it open with a creak.

The smell hit her first, a pungent blend of wet soil and rotting vegetation, quickly overpowered by the heavy stench of spent flowers.

As the door opened fully, she saw the Garden.

This was no manicured lawn with pruned trees and tamed flower beds as depicted in every artistic rendering of Adam and Eve in Paradise. This was an underground rainforest, an abundance of color and growth, teeming with life. This was Nature unbound.

A shaft of light shone down from an aperture high above the soaring roof of the cave, alighting on an immense tree in its center. Crevices and deep cracks riddled its thick trunk, big enough to shelter a human within. Its branches reached high above and out across the cave, protecting myriad species beneath its leafy boughs.

As Morgan looked up at the ancient tree, a sense of awe rose within. Her life was truly insignificant in the face of its majesty, a brief flicker of light in a galaxy of stars. She had felt this before in the presence of vast natural beauty, but there was something wild about this tree, something untamed and fierce.

As she stared into the heart of the green, a deep knowledge stirred in some kind of collective memory. The air shimmered and Morgan saw herself dancing with a group of women under the full moon, wreathed in ivy and flowers, worshipping the Mother Goddess together. They circled around the tree, spinning faster, heads thrown back in ecstasy, intoxicated by the sap that was both poison and drug.

A man stepped from the shadows, his eyes wide at the sight of the wild gathering.

A hiss from the women. *Trespasser.*

They ran at him as one, teeth bared, whipped into a frenzy. The first bowled him over and the others tore at his flesh, beating him and ripping at his skin until there was nothing left but a grisly corpse.

The women smeared his blood on their skin and used it to paint the trunk of the tree with ancient symbols. This was the domain of Eve, and Adam had no place in it.

Morgan gasped, and she was back in the cave again, surrounded by the monks who controlled the Garden—or at least, who tried. But she sensed that this place could not be controlled for long. Eden was no paradise for humanity.

"It's the Tree of Life," Aurelia whispered like a prayer. She walked toward the door with hesitant steps, a smile on her lips, her eyes filled with wonder.

She stepped over the threshold into the Garden, her first footstep on the soil of this holy place.

A vine shot out and wrapped itself around her ankle, digging into her flesh with razor-sharp barbs.

Aurelia screamed in horror and tried to step back through the door.

Jake ran forward to help, but two of the monks stopped him at sword-point.

"She asked for this," the Abbot said, his eyes alight with anticipation. "Now she will understand what the Garden truly is."

The vine jerked back inside, pulling Aurelia to the ground. She screamed and scrabbled at the dirt, desperately trying to get back to the cave.

Two more barbed vines squirmed across the ground and

wrapped themselves around her body. One encircled her neck, choking off her screams, and they dragged her back into the impenetrable green toward the Tree of Life. Her muffled cries died to silence as more wicked vines wrapped her body tight until there was no way the heiress could breathe anymore.

Aurelia's corpse, now a cocoon of jungle green, rose up through the lower boughs of the tree, hoisted by monstrous lianas until it reached the fork of a branch.

Cracks in the living wood opened up to receive the sacrifice, crushing what was left of the heiress as the vines fed the tree its bloody offering. The sound of cracking bone, creaking wood and the rustling of vegetation filled the Garden and then it was over. Nothing left but bright blood mingled with sap dripping down the trunk.

The horror of it threatened to overwhelm Morgan. She had seen death in many guises, but this seemed an abomination, even as she understood that all must return to Nature in the end. After everything that humanity did to destroy the Earth, perhaps it was the most natural thing in the world for Eden to fight back.

"This is the truth of the Garden," the Abbot said. "Mankind was kept from the Tree of Life for good reason. Nature unfettered is Nature ascendant and She will devour the Earth if we allow Her to. The Order has spent generations ensuring She remains tamed and our sacred duty is to protect humanity from Nature unbound."

He pointed at the bloody stains on the trunk. "We knew of the mission of Aurelia dos Santos Fidalgo. With her wealth and desire to honor Nature above all, even at the cost of our entire species, she was a threat to our sacred purpose." He sighed. "But perhaps she realized her mistake in those final moments."

The Abbot stepped closer to the altar, placed a hand on Camara's brow and stroked the blood-matted hair back from her face. "This one, too, has been a threat. Now she must face the Garden she has sought for so long."

CHAPTER 22

AT THE ABBOT'S WORDS, Morgan looked over at Jake. They had to stop this now, but there was little they could do against the gathered monks with their swords.

Jake gave an obvious glance sideways at one of the heavy candelabra topped with lighted candles. It was the closest thing to a weapon. She could reach it if he caused a distraction. Morgan nodded imperceptibly and readied herself for action.

A sudden shout and a monk darted forward to the door, his sword raised.

He chopped at one of the barbed vines that snaked its way out of the door. None of the other monks reacted, and the Abbot looked unsurprised at first. Clearly the Garden testing its limits was not an unusual occurrence.

But then the sound of rustling grew louder, quickly joined by a rumble of soil pushed aside and the ripping of plants uprooted.

The Abbot frowned. "Quick! Shut the door," he shouted in alarm.

Two more monks jumped forward to push at the ancient portal.

A horde of vines exploded from the undergrowth.

They slithered fast as snakes, some across the floor, some around the edges of the door. An immense mass of them, tumbling and teeming, as thick as a man's arm, each slashing the air with thorns tipped with poison.

The weight of the plants thrust the door wide as more of them joined the attack. The monks weren't strong enough, and the ancient portal swung fully open.

One monk went down, his screams quickly muffled by a bulky tendril that thrust down his throat, cracking his jaw and writhing within his torso before smashing out of his rib cage in a bloody burst.

Jake darted forward and grabbed the dead monk's sword, joining the others against a common foe.

The Abbot retreated, his face a mask of despair, as the Brothers hacked and chopped at the writhing undergrowth. But the sheer volume of deadly plants overwhelmed them, squirming and twitching through the cave.

One vine reached the narrow corridor to the giant statues and slithered inside. A monk ran to head it off, guarding the exit as he slashed and cut, trying to stop the Garden finding a way out into the world above. The vines came at him thick and fast, wrapping themselves around his legs faster than he could cut them away.

Eden would soon escape its prison.

"There is only one way left," the Abbot shouted above the crack of branches and the rustle of thick stems. "Brothers, you know what we must do. Be strong in your duty."

The remaining monks around the cavern gave up trying to chop at the wild vines and ran for the huge wooden barrels that lay against the rocky walls.

Two of them pulled the lid off one and tipped it over.

A slick of petrol ran across the floor and ignited in the fire pit. The vines closest to it jerked away, but the dark liquid quickly coated the green surface. Stinking fumes permeated the cavern as other Brothers tipped over more vats until the stone floor ran ankle deep with flammable liquid and the flames began to spread.

While Jake slashed at the slithering vines with their sharp thorns, Morgan clambered up onto the stone altar and pulled Camara close. The professor shivered in a fever, her skin burning up from poison that had seeped into her flesh. If she didn't get medical help soon, she would die of infection, but it looked like they would all perish in the fire before then. The monks would burn the Garden to ash rather than let it escape.

Despite the noise and fury around them, Morgan found a calm at the heart of the storm, a sense of peace in this ancient place. There truly was a Garden of Eden, a place where Nature ruled, but it was not a haven for humanity. It could truly be their end.

The knowledge that Nature could be both good and evil, healer and killer, was a truth denied by so many, and yet here, it seemed simple to understand. In the end, Nature would always win, and the corpses of all who stood against Her would be food for Her next generation.

A bellow rang out across the chamber.

One monk called to God as he ladled petrol over himself, soaking his tunic. He struck his sword, turning it to flame and setting himself alight at the same time.

He howled a final prayer and ran headlong through the ancient wooden door into the Garden. The vines ripped at him, but he made it to the Tree, wrapping his arms around it so his flaming corpse charred at its bark.

The other remaining Brothers around the chamber followed suit, dousing themselves in flammable liquid, faces set with determination, hands clutching the swords with which they would fight to the death.

The Abbot stood watching, his old frame bent over his sword, his eyes betraying a deep sadness. He edged around the cavern to the altar through the wash of petrol, his gaze fixed on Morgan.

When he reached the altar, he leaned in to whisper for her ears only. "Our mission has been the same for generations. To keep the Garden from the world or destroy Her with our last breath." He held his sword up, a wiry strength left in his failing limbs. "I will die with my Brothers, but you must live."

He pointed to a side chamber. "There's a tunnel back up to the surface. Go that way before the flames consume everything." He pulled at the neck of his tunic to reveal a silver pendant and tugged it over his head. The Abbot took one last look, then gave it to Morgan. "Take this to the Order at the monastery of Adana in Turkey. Please, I beg you. This incarnation of the Garden must perish but it cannot be the end."

Morgan attached the pendant around her neck and hid it under her jacket. "What is it?"

Tears welled in the Abbot's eyes and rolled down his cheeks. "The last Seed from the Tree of Life. From this, She can grow again. There have been many Gardens over millennia, each destroyed by man and each grown again. The Tree is not life for humanity. It is life for Nature. It can spread faster than anything you've seen and is strengthened by blood sacrifice. Aurelia was right — given free rein, it would transform the Earth into Eden once more, and in that Garden, there is no place for mankind."

He clutched at Morgan's hand. "You are the only way for the Seed to pass out of here. We will all die with this Garden, as is our vow. The place is mined to ensure its destruction. But you must escape, and the Seed must be protected. Go now."

The Abbot turned away from the altar and stepped over the writhing vines to a heavy lever on the wall. He pushed it down.

A clunk. A grinding of stone on sand.

Liquid spurted down in a fine rain from the cave roof above. Not water, but more fuel.

The Abbot faced the fiery inferno that the Garden had become. He held his sword high and struck it to ignite the flames. With a cry to God, the Abbot ran with all his strength toward the Tree of Life.

He fought through the vines with energy far greater than his age should allow, his faith sustaining him as thorns ripped at his flesh. His body ran with blood, but still he pressed on as the flames rose higher around him.

With the last of his strength, the old man stabbed his blade into the heart of the Tree even as its bark opened up to consume him.

Morgan jumped off the altar and Jake rushed to hoist Camara over his broad shoulders in a firefighter's lift. They ran for the side chamber and darted up the staircase.

A boom came from the cavern behind, then a whooshing sound.

The ground shook.

Morgan clutched at the wall of the staircase as chunks of rock fell down from the ceiling above. As the shudder passed by, she ran again, taking two steps at a time, Jake close behind with Camara.

As the stairs wound up and out of the caves, the sound of rumbling pursued them. The very heart of the mountain began to collapse under their feet.

Morgan sprinted, her breath ragged, grateful for her recent training, and glad that Jake was there to carry Camara. She could not do this alone.

Together they made it out of the mouth of the staircase and onto the opposite side of the volcano from the cave descent.

"Keep going," Jake shouted as they emerged into the dusk.

Together, they ran down the slope of the volcano, across the meadow beyond.

Another boom. Bigger this time.

An underground explosion ripped through the fabric of the mountain, shaking the ground as if the cherubim awoke from their ancient sleep to wield fire against the trespassers of Eden.

CHAPTER 23

THE BLAST THREW THEM off their feet. Morgan instinctively rolled to soften her landing. Jake took the force of the fall to protect Camara and landed hard against some rocks with a groan.

A crevasse opened up behind them and a fiery pillar twisted into the sky as if reaching toward Heaven. It burned with the colors of the Garden, the bright carnelian and violet of its flowers with forest green at its heart, washed with the blood of those it devoured.

Morgan scrambled over to Jake. "Are you alright?"

He groaned and rolled onto his back. "Just about. But I don't think I can carry the professor much further."

Camara lay prone next to him, her eyelids fluttering, still deep in a fever.

Morgan stood up, testing her strength as she looked back at the chasm, a fresh scar on an ancient mountain. The monks had mined it well. Everything was gone, burned to ash. But something about that ancient tree made her think that perhaps something remained under it all, and life would rise again from the embers. Nature always found a way.

"Hello! Mr Jake!"

The voice came from lower down the mountain. Morgan turned to see Darius with his donkey and she sighed with relief. They would have much to explain but at least they had a way out of here and ARKANE's budget would go a long way to making this whole situation just a natural occurrence in a faraway corner of the world.

As they waited for Darius to reach them, Morgan took Camara's hand. The professor had spent a lifetime searching for Eden, and it had almost killed her. Aurelia and the Brotherhood had perished at its heart. The Garden was no haven, and the expulsion from Eden, whether myth or history, was clearly for good reason.

The silver pendant around her neck lay heavy on her skin, the Seed inside a potential threat to humanity. The Abbot had charged her with taking it to the Adana monastery, to give to the Brothers to keep safe from the world. But would it be better off in the vaults of ARKANE far away from religious fanatics? Or were even they enough to hold its terrifying potential in check?

Morgan thought of the ecological groups who believed humanity to be a stain upon the Earth, that Nature would do better without their species. Those people would love to get their hands on the Seed. Some part of her even wanted to see what would happen if it was planted, whether it truly would take over the Earth in a new Eden, or find itself tamed in a far different environment than its former incarnations.

There were many possible futures for the Seed, but she had one idea that seemed the safest. A way to preserve it far away from humanity's worst intentions.

* * *

Svalbard, Norway. One week later.

The military plane touched down just after a storm had passed. The sky was washed clean, and the sun shone against the ice-blue fjord that flowed out into the Greenland Sea.

Clouds whipped past high above in the grey sky and a biting wind chilled Morgan to the bone, even through her insulated jacket. She hurried over to the snowmobile, backpack securely in place, revved up the vehicle and crossed the snowy peninsula to her final destination.

Svalbard was a remote archipelago in the Arctic Ocean, north of mainland Europe and halfway to the North Pole. It really was the edge of the world and difficult to get to, even in decent weather.

Martin Klein had arranged Morgan's trip, hiding her itinerary from the public record and even from Director Marietti and Jake. Something about her vision of the women in the cave made Morgan uneasy about anyone knowing of the potential of the Seed. Camara and Sebastian were recovering well — and seeing a lot of each other, apparently — and the Garden was gone, but she didn't feel that the mission was over yet. This would hopefully be the last stop on her journey.

There were nearly two thousand different seed banks around the world with teams that collected and preserved samples from every eco-system. The Svalbard Seed Bank was a backup of genetic material in one of the most remote places on Earth, in case natural or human-driven disaster destroyed any of the others. Some seed banks had already been lost in Iraq and Afghanistan and many considered this place to be one of the most secure due to its remoteness.

A wedge-shaped metal structure emerged from the ice with a square array of mirrors at the top and stainless steel panels reflecting the turquoise sky. A narrow bridge led over the icy ground to the double-paneled steel doors, a modest entrance to what many considered a Doomsday Vault, a place that may one day save humanity. A fitting home for the Seed.

As Morgan pulled up on the snowmobile, one door opened and a huge man peered out. "Welcome, Dr Sierra. Come on in."

The head scientist, Kristofer Rubeck, was not quite what Morgan had expected. He towered over her, his frame dwarfing hers. With his thick ginger hair and bushy beard, Kristofer was the very image of a Norse explorer from ancient times. Yet his long fingers were slender and delicate, necessary for his precise work with fragile ecology.

Morgan followed him inside and Kristofer closed the enormous steel door behind them, the clang echoing through the corridor that led into the heart of the ice mountain.

"There are many millions of seeds here," Kristofer explained. "From almost a million different varieties of food crops. Thirteen thousand years of agricultural history that perhaps, one day, will save the whole of humanity." He gave a cheeky grin. "Or at least some of its eco-systems."

"What do you mean?" Morgan asked.

Kristofer shrugged. "To be honest, an apocalyptic event will kill us all and no one is going to care about this seed bank at the end of the world. But localized catastrophes happen all the time, miniature Doomsdays that end natural environments — war, floods, fire, mining, even human choice over some strains rather than others. One of our goals is to protect genetic material from all areas of the world. You never know, one of these seeds may be the answer to a question we don't even know how to ask yet."

As Kristofer led the way down the long metal tunnel, one hundred and fifty meters into the mountain, Morgan reflected on his words. Did the Seed from the Tree of Life contain genetic data that could help people right now? Was she doing the right thing by hiding it here? Perhaps she should take it to a lab and have it tested for anything that might be useful to humanity?

But then she remembered her vision in the cavern, the wild women who tore a man apart, and the tree that feasted on blood and thrived on sacrifice. Humanity was cast out of Eden for their own protection, and even now, the world wasn't ready for the knowledge of what the Tree of Life could do. Perhaps one day, but for now, the Seed must rest here, far from those who would turn Her loose to destroy or try to tame Her for their own purposes.

They emerged from the tunnel into a long main chamber with three doors. A thin layer of ice lay on the outside of the middle entrance, hinting at the temperature inside.

"Only one of the vaults is used right now," Kristofer explained. "But hopefully, we'll fill them all over time."

He indicated a metal table in the middle of the room with a neat pile of silver packets, test tubes and a vacuum packing machine. "It's not too complicated. We pack the seeds carefully and then store them at sub-zero temperatures." He smiled, brimming over with enthusiasm for his chosen field of expertise. "But think about it. Seeds are the basis for everything. What we eat, what we wear, the very fabric of life. We have to protect them, for our own sakes."

Morgan exhaled slowly as tension seeped from her body. Kristofer's words made her confident that this was the right place to leave the Seed. She opened her backpack, pulled out a clear plastic bag and placed it on the metal table.

The Seed was small enough to cup in her palm and shaped like the curve of a kidney bean or the spine of an embryo. Its surface was silvery grey and slightly pitted, a hard shell that protected the genetic riches within. This tiny package was Nature's perfect way to preserve and pass itself down to the next generation.

Kristofer bent over the bag, a crease forming between his eyebrows as he considered the Seed. "It's a tree of some kind, but this pitting has some similarities to poppy, even some fruits. It's also akin to some resurrection plants." He looked up at Morgan. "They feign death for years but can rehydrate to full function. Do you know what it is?"

She shook her head. "I don't know exactly, but it was given to me in the mountains of north-western Iran before a volcanic eruption destroyed the area. The eco-system is gone, and this is all that remains."

"It's the only one?"

Morgan nodded. "As far as I know."

"Then it will be safe here until it's needed once more." Kristofer pulled on a pair of gloves and carefully opened the bag. He lifted out the Seed and placed it on a sterile surface, took several photos and then packed it inside one of the silver bags.

As he sealed it with a delicate finger, Morgan's heart beat faster. Part of her wanted to reach out and snatch it back, keep it close to her. The Seed still wanted to be free.

She clenched her fists, restrained her urge and watched as Kristofer noted the number on the silver packet and typed a description into the computer log.

"That's it," he said. "Now I just need to put it in the vault. I'll catalogue it alongside other Iranian material."

He pulled on a heavier jacket and thicker gloves and carried the silver packet to the door of the vault. "You'll have to stay out here, but you can catch a glimpse inside as I open the door."

Morgan stood with her back against the wall of the main chamber, her breath frosting in the air. As the cold seeped through her padded jacket, she became aware of the thousands of tons of rock and ice above her and the millions of precious seeds in the vault beyond. She was truly insignificant against the vast timescale of the Earth, and that thought was strangely comforting.

Kristofer opened the vault door. Tall metal shelves laden with boxes stretched toward an ice-covered ceiling, each labeled with letters and numbers with no sign of the true nature of what lay inside.

As the door slammed shut and Kristofer disappeared from sight, Morgan smiled. Humanity protected a future Eden here in the ice, and now the Seed lay within its safe haven at last. It instinctively knew how to wait. The life inside would lie dormant until conditions allowed it to grow once more in a perfect alignment of light, temperature and moisture. It waited in the dark to live, while humanity existed in the light, waiting to die.

Morgan walked away, down the long corridor and back out into the Arctic sun, ready for a new day.

* * *

THE END

ENJOYED TREE OF LIFE?

If you loved the book and have a moment to spare, I would really appreciate a short review on the page where you bought the book. Your help in spreading the word is gratefully appreciated and reviews make a huge difference to helping new readers find the series. Thank you!

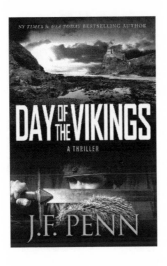

Get a free copy of the bestselling thriller, *Day of the Vikings*, ARKANE book 5, when you sign up to join my Reader's Group. You'll also be notified of new releases, giveaways and receive personal updates from behind the scenes of my thrillers.

WWW.JFPENN.COM/FREE

*   *   *

Day of the Vikings, an ARKANE thriller

A ritual murder on a remote island under the shifting skies of the aurora borealis.

A staff of power that can summon Ragnarok, the Viking apocalypse.

When Neo-Viking terrorists invade the British Museum in London to reclaim the staff of Skara Brae, ARKANE agent Dr. Morgan Sierra is trapped in the building along with hostages under mortal threat.

As the slaughter begins, Morgan works alongside psychic Blake Daniel to discern the past of the staff, dating back to islands invaded by the Vikings generations ago.

Can Morgan and Blake uncover the truth before Ragnarok is unleashed, consuming all in its wake?

Day of the Vikings is a fast-paced, supernatural thriller set in London and the islands of Orkney, Lindisfarne and Iona. Set in the present day, it resonates with the history and myth of the Vikings.

If you love an action-packed thriller,
you can get Day of the Vikings for free now:

WWW.JFPENN.COM/FREE

Day of the Vikings features Dr. Morgan Sierra from the ARKANE thrillers, and Blake Daniel from the London Crime Thrillers, but it is also a stand-alone novella that can be read and enjoyed separately.

AUTHOR'S NOTE

I hope you enjoyed this adventure with Morgan and Jake. I had fun putting it together, and I learned a lot along the way. One of my favorite aspects of being an author is the research, and I certainly loved this one! As ever, I try to stick to the truth as much as possible in terms of locations and historical events and then spin that into a story.

Ets Haim Portuguese Synagogue, Amsterdam, Netherlands

I recommend visiting the synagogue if you're in the city. It's truly a beautiful place, and I would never wish to see it harmed. Quite the opposite. I believe that stories can highlight places that deserve more attention and protection, and I write about the synagogue (and all my locations) with that intent.

You can find more at www.esnoga.com and www.etshaimmanuscripts.nl

You can see pictures from my Amsterdam research trip at www.booksandtravel.page/unusual-amsterdam

I also found an intriguing book in their fantastic store, *Jewish Pirates of the Caribbean* by Edward Kritzler. This unusual title sparked my imagination and led to the scenes on the island of Jamaica.

Lisbon

We had a wonderful long weekend in Lisbon, relaxing in the glorious weather, and yes, enjoying several *pastéis de nata* in Belém! They're definitely my favorite pastries. You can find pictures and recommendations from our trip here: www.booksandtravel.page/lisbon

Macau

I picked Macau as a setting because of the ruins of St Paul's, and I wanted to show the extent of the Portuguese Empire. I was stunned to find that there really is a Tree of Life engraved on the facade. This kind of synchronicity often happens in my book research process, where I think I am writing fiction, but then real life happens to fit with my story.

Brazil

Aurelia's family mine is based on the Carajás Mine, the largest iron ore mine in the world.

The synagogue in Recife is considered the oldest in the Americas, but the Museum of the Inquisition is actually in Belo Horizonte, not Recife. I didn't want to add another Brazilian location to the story, so I moved it. The details of the museum are accurate based on researching through the site www.museudainquisicao.org.br

The locations in Rio de Janeiro are as accurate as possible and there are indeed hatches leading onto the top of Christ the Redeemer, although access is not available to the public. I based the scene on photos taken by travel blogger, Lee Thompson, who gained special access during the World Cup.

Location of the Garden of Eden

It's fascinating to read research from different perspectives, and there were two books that primarily informed the possible locations.

History of Paradise: The Garden of Eden in Myth and Tradition by Jean Delumeau and *Legend: The Genesis of Civilisation* by David Rohl. The latter book is the primary source for the location I decided on.

I would love to visit Tabriz one day, along with Isfahan and the other incredible sites of Iran. It's on my list, but I haven't been yet, so these scenes are written entirely from books and online research.

Svalbard

I based this chapter on a *Time* magazine article about the real Seed Vault: Time.com/doomsday-vault

Thoughts on Nature

I love being in nature, but we live in a world where ecological catastrophe seems closer every day. The dichotomy at the heart of Eden is real, and this book is all about balancing the things that seem impossible to balance.

Aurelia believes that the natural world would be better off without humanity, whereas the Order acknowledges Nature's destructive potential and wants to protect mankind from it while also exploiting its resources.

I love the natural world and want to protect it, but I also believe that humanity is a valuable part of the biosphere and has the potential to fix the problems that face us all. I highly recommend reading *Novacene: The Coming Age of Hyperintelligence* by James Lovelock, the original proponent of the Gaia hypothesis, and his thoughts on how we might save the planet from ecological collapse.

During the process of writing this book, I learned of the rate of destruction of trees and donated to The Woodland Trust, woodlandtrust.org.uk and The Tree Council, treecouncil.org.uk

Wicked Plants by Amy Stewart inspired the deadly possibilities of the Order's garden and author J.T. Croft made sure the botanical aspects were as accurate as can be in a novel.

Morgan's vision of the women at the Tree is based on *The Bacchae*, a Greek tragedy by Euripides. I saw the play in my teens and have never forgotten the bloody rage of the women in their violent frenzy.

Bibliography

Conquerors: How Portugal Forged the First Global Empire — Roger Crowley

Ets Haim: 18 Highlights from the Oldest Jewish Library in the World — Emile Schrijver & Heide Warncke

Evil Roots: Killer Tales of the Botanical Gothic — Edited by Daisy Butcher

History of Paradise: The Garden of Eden in Myth and Tradition — Jean Delumeau

Jewish Pirates of the Caribbean: How a Generation of Swashbuckling Jews Carved Out an Empire in the New World in Their Quest for Treasure, Religious Freedom — and Revenge — Edward Kritzler

Lab Girl: A Story of Trees, Science and Love — Hope Jahren

Legend: The Genesis of Civilisation — David Rohl

Novacene: The Coming Age of Hyperintelligence — James Lovelock

The Last Kabbalist of Lisbon — Richard Zimler. I read this book many years ago, and it inspired thoughts of Jewish history and the rich traditions of Portugal decades before I visited the country itself.

You can also listen to an interview I did with Richard about his books at www.booksandtravel.page/richard-zimler

The Bacchae — *Euripides*

The Portuguese: A Modern History — Barry Hatton

The Portuguese Jews of Jamaica — Mordechai Arbell

Wicked Plants: The A–Z of Plants That Kill, Maim, Intoxicate and Otherwise Offend — Amy Stewart

ACKNOWLEDGMENTS

Thanks to my readers who continue to buy my books and enable me to keep researching the fascinating history and places behind the ARKANE adventures!

Thanks to Jen Blood, my fantastic first reader and story editor, for her continued insights. Thanks to author J.T. Croft for his botanical expertise, and to Wendy Janes for another great proofread.

Thanks to Jane Dixon Smith for the cover design and print formatting.

MORE BOOKS BY J.F.PENN

Thanks for joining Morgan, Jake and the
ARKANE team. The adventures continue …

Brooke and Daniel Psychological/Crime Thrillers

Mapwalker Dark Fantasy Adventures

More Books and Short Stories

Risen Gods

The Dark Queen

A Thousand Fiendish Angels:
Short stories based on Dante's Inferno

More books coming soon ...

You can sign up to be notified of new releases, giveaways
and pre-release specials - plus, get a free book!

www.JFPenn.com/free

If you loved the book and have a moment to spare, I would
really appreciate a short review on the page where you
bought the book. Your help in spreading the word is gratefully appreciated and reviews make a huge difference to
helping new readers find the series.

Thank you!

ABOUT J.F. PENN

J.F. Penn is the Award-nominated, New York Times and USA Today bestselling author of the ARKANE action adventure thrillers, Brooke & Daniel Psychological Thrillers, and the Mapwalker fantasy adventure series, as well as other stand-alone stories.

Her books weave together ancient artifacts, relics of power, international locations and adventure with an edge of the supernatural. Joanna lives in Bath, England and enjoys a nice G&T.

You can follow Joanna's book research and travels on Instagram and Facebook @jfpennauthor and also on her podcast at BooksAndTravel.page or on your favorite podcast app.

* * *

Sign up for your free thriller, *Day of the Vikings*, and updates from behind the scenes, research, and giveaways at:

www.JFPenn.com/free

* * *

Connect with Joanna:
www.JFPenn.com
joanna@JFPenn.com
www.Facebook.com/JFPennAuthor
www.Instagram.com/JFPennAuthor
www.BooksAndTravel.page

* * *

For writers:

Joanna's site, www.TheCreativePenn.com empowers authors with the knowledge they need to choose their creative future. Books and courses by Joanna Penn, as well as the award-winning *Creative Penn Podcast* provide information and inspiration on how to write, publish and market books, and make a living as a writer.

Made in the USA
Middletown, DE
15 December 2020